The Christmas Wedding

A complete list of books by James Patterson is at the end of this book. For previews of upcoming books and more information about James Patterson, please visit JamesPatterson.com or find him on Facebook or at your app store.

The Christmas Wedding

JAMES PATTERSON *and*

RICHARD DiLALLO

DOUBLEDAY LARGE PRINT HOME LIBRARY EDITION

Ⓛ Ⓑ

Little, Brown and Company

NEW YORK   BOSTON   LONDON

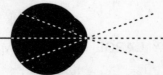

This Large Print Book carries the
Seal of Approval of N.A.V.H.

For the four corners of my world:
Emma, Jonny, Max, Nick
—RDL

The Christmas Wedding

THE INVITATION LIST

THE BRIDE

GABY SUMMERHILL, fifty-four, teacher, mother of four, widow for three years, lives in Stockbridge, Massachusetts

GABY'S FAMILY

CLAIRE DONOGHUE, Gaby's daughter, thirty-five, married, lives in Myrtle Beach, South Carolina
HANK DONOGHUE, Claire's husband, thirty-four
GUS, their son, fourteen

TOBY and **GABRIELLE,** their eleven-year-old twins

EMILY SUMMERHILL, Gaby's youngest daughter, twenty-nine, lawyer in Manhattan

BART DeFRANCO, Emily's husband, twenty-nine, resident in neurology

SETH SUMMERHILL, Gaby's only son, twenty-six, novelist, lives in Boston

ANDIE COLLINS, Seth's girlfriend, twenty-four, commercial artist

LIZZIE RODGERS, Gaby's daughter, thirty-four, married, works part time at Walmart, lives near Gaby

MIKE RODGERS, Lizzie's husband, thirty-six

TALLULAH, their daughter, eight

GABY'S SUITORS

TOM HAYDEN, fifty-four, owns a farm, former pro hockey player, grew up with Gaby

JACOB COLEMAN, fifty-two, rabbi at a temple in Stockbridge

MARTIN SUMMERHILL, fifty-five, Gaby's brother-in-law

PROLOGUE

You're Invited, or Else

GABY'S FIRST VIDEO

Only twenty-four days until Christmas, and this Christmas is going to be one you won't forget.

Need proof? I think I can give you proof.

I want all four of you to take a good, long look at the screen and your mom.

Everybody watching? Emily? Claire? Seth? Lizzie? *Emily?* You see anything unusual or, well, kind of stunning?

Okay. Let me turn around for you . . . Turning . . . Turning again.

Yes. Your eyes tell the truth. *I have lost twelve pounds and several ounces.*

Stop, stop! No worries, no frets or fears. No neurotic theories about my health.

I'm not sick or anything like that. Maybe a little sick in the head. As always. Part of my charm.

I just gave up Ben & Jerry's Chocolate Chip Cookie Dough and the occasional beer before bedtime. And I banished mayonnaise—low-fat or otherwise—from the house. And white bread. Dunkin' Donuts for sure. It made me somewhat miserable . . . and hungry. But it also made me thinner. And, I must admit, happier. Yes, I'm happier than I've been in a long time.

I needed a big change. Everybody needs a change. If you don't change, you're stuck in a rut.

I know that people around here always say, "Oh, Gaby, you lead such an interesting life . . . You run that farm of yours pretty much by yourself. You write a food blog that isn't too egotistical or boring. You teach the local kids to read and write."

Oh, yes, I do . . . and I love it . . . but honestly, it just wasn't enough for me.

I was in a life rut that was only getting deeper. R-u-t. Put on boots and a loden coat the morning after a snowstorm and trudge to the henhouse to collect four eggs. Start adding nutritional facts to the recipes on the blog and people you never even met accuse you of being a nutrition Nazi.

Teach English, or at least try to make the kids love reading. I know this is going to come as a bit of a shock, but most teenagers think that *Great Expectations*—to use a phrase—"blows," but that any book with a vampire in it is brilliant. Especially if the vampire is darkly handsome and promises eternal love with every bite. *Great Expectations* does kind of blow, by the way.

So anyway, I promise you, I'm not going through the dreaded midlife crisis. I'm not even *at* my midlife.

And, hey, the first one of you who makes a crack about my being way *past* midlife gets tossed out of the will. I'm serious, kiddies.

I do need some excitement, though. I think the wildest thing I've done in the last three years is to ask your kids to call me by my first name. I disliked being called Grandma. Made me itchy all over.

Back to the subject . . . I've lost twelve pounds.

After all . . .

I want to be able to fit into my wedding gown.

Anyone who's fainted should please get up off the floor. And don't start telephoning one another until this video is over.

Yes, you heard right. I said *wedding gown.* As in *wedding.* As in *bride.* As in *wedding in our barn.*

You're looking at the bride right now, and she's actually smiling. She's happy. Very much so. You know I don't complain, but there was a long, dark time after your father died and I'm finally out of that black hole.

You're probably wondering who the lucky groom is. Well, as you used to say when you were just little brats, that's for me to know and you to find out.

Everybody is coming home to Stockbridge for Christmas. Claire, Emily, Seth, and Lizzie. You and your children, your spouses, your lovers, dogs, cats, who-

ever and whatever. We haven't been together as a family since your dad died.

So it's Christmas in Stockbridge.

Then you'll find out who the lucky
man is. Till then. I love you. And I'm so
happy I almost can't believe it.

See you at Christmas . . . when all will
be revealed.

BOOK ONE

Christmas Dreaming

Chapter 1

CLAIRE AND HANK

Claire Donoghue, Gaby's eldest daughter, had just finished her mother's video, and, well, *wow.* Go, Gaby! For the moment, though, Claire was paying her household bills, and bill paying was kind of like playing "I love you, I love you not" with hand grenades. Sooner or later, Claire knew, one of them was going to blow up in her face. In everybody's face.

"I love you, South Carolina Electric and Gas," she said, placing that bill in the stack she intended to pay.

"I love you not, emergency root canal."

It was as good a system as any for deciding how to parcel out their slim income to pay the usual fat stack of bills. It was only during the luckiest of months that Hank's money from construction work, and Claire's income from tutoring, covered most of the bills. This was not one of those months.

Claire sat at a small, wobbly oak table in the chilly sunroom. She wore two Shetland sweaters in two different shades of dark blue, white painter's pants, and fingerless woolen gloves. She called her style cheap cute. And, in fact, Claire was cute. Even after three kids, she was still holding her own—pug nose rather than spreading pig nose, smattering of freckles, short reddish-brown hair, "girlish" figure.

The truth was, though, she felt anything but cute; she felt tired and rundown. She felt like total crap, and nobody knew it, and nobody much cared.

James Taylor was playing softly on Claire's laptop. She liked James okay, always had.

I've seen fire and I've seen rain.

Claire knew what he was singing about. She gazed out of the sunroom and although their house was three blocks from the beach, she could see a sliver of the gray December ocean. The sand was cold and the horizon lifeless. Myrtle Beach, South Carolina, was a summer hot spot, but for Claire and Hank Donoghue it was their year-round home. That meant that when the tourists left and the cheesy concession stands closed down and the splintery boardwalk was deserted—well, that meant that Claire and Hank were left with each other. And that wasn't always a good thing. Not for the past few years. And definitely not today. Hank just kept getting worse and worse and worse.

"Hey, babe," she heard him call from his downstairs den. "Can you bring me a big coldy-oldy tea and maybe-baby some Eyetalian crackers?"

Claire knew he was asking for an iced tea and Pepperidge Farm Milano cookies. She also realized, from his ridiculous language, that he was stoned out of his mind.

"In a minute," she called. She *did not*

want a fight today. Or any day, really. She couldn't stand his blowups, but she didn't know what to do about them. The kids loved Hank.

She stood up, but she couldn't stop obsessing about the video from her mom—the one that had knocked the wind out of her. So, Gaby was getting married. That was pretty terrific. But her mom wouldn't say to whom. Just when and where. Christmas Day back home in Massachusetts at their farm. Gaby loved her mysteries.

"Hey, Claire, where's the grub?" Hank shouted again.

Claire rolled her eyes and headed for the kitchen. She couldn't help thinking that her mom would never, *ever* fetch coldy-oldies for her father—and her father would never have asked, certainly never have shouted up from the basement.

Keep the peace, Claire, she reminded herself. *Only twenty-four days until Christmas.*

Chapter 2

But this craziness with Hank had to stop real soon, Claire was thinking. She could suck it up until the new year, for better or worse, for poorer or poorer, but then Hank had to get his act together and find a real, full-time job. No more excuses; no more softball games, flag-football games, or golf with his buddies three times a week.

Claire's overarching worry as she carried the snacks down to the den was that she might get a contact high from inhaling the gauzy clouds of weed that Hank had already generated in there.

She also marveled at what a multitasker her husband was. He was resting on a faded foldout couch watching a Falcons-Saints game while listening to Radiohead blasting from speakers on the bookshelf. Oh, yeah, and he was occasionally glancing at an article in *Wired.*

She studied Hank for a moment, trying to be objective. Talk about cute. In spite of the dirty matted blond hair, the two days of stubble, and the emerging potbelly, you couldn't miss the handsome farm boy hiding not too far underneath. Even the wardrobe was perfect: worn jeans, work boots, a worn-out blue-and-green-patterned flannel shirt.

"God, Hank, I don't know what smells more—you or the pot smoke," she said with a forced smile, setting a bag of Milano cookies and a huge glass of iced tea on the floor next to him.

"I was playing Sunday football, you get . . . you know . . . just get off my ass, will you . . . Like . . . just get . . . ," he said, working hard to put together a coherent string of words.

"I have some good news," Claire said.

"You won the South Carolina lottery?"

"No. That's not it."

"Then why do I care?"

He was clearly in one of his sonofa-bitch moods, but she was determined to tell him her news. It had brightened Claire's day, actually, made her laugh out loud.

"I got one of those videos from my mom . . ."

Hank immediately began a bad and mean-spirited imitation of Gaby: "Oh, I'm so busy. I'm finding a cure for leuke-mia. I'm saving the rain forest. Me and my friends are feeding twelve-grain toast to the homeless of western Mass—"

"Stop it. That's totally unfair," Claire said. "Can I talk for a second here? *Can I talk?*"

To her surprise, Hank stopped. Maybe she'd confused him by interrupt-ing his rant.

"My mom is getting married."

Hank chuckled.

"Who's the lucky fella? I know, what's-his-name—Mark Harmon, right? Tom Cruise?"

"You're hilarious. Mom says she'll tell us at Christmas when we all go up there."

Hank's face fell, but not in a funny way.

"Yeah, well, I'm not snowplowing my way up to Massachusetts the day before Christmas," he said.

"My mom is getting married *on Christmas.*"

"It's just some trick of hers to get everyone together at her farm. One big happy family."

"Maybe that *is* part of the plan. So? It's been almost three years since my dad died. The family hasn't been together since the day we buried him. My mother was in a dark place for a few years."

Hank tried another approach.

"C'mon, if you're up in Stockbridge for Christmas, who's going to tutor those colored kids you're so involved with? The retards that you spend so much time with?"

"First of all, two of the kids are white. Two are black, and those *African-American* children are classmates of *our* chil-

dren, you asshole. I help them because . . ."

"What did you call me?" he yelled.
Then he stood up unsteadily. Claire
didn't like this. His face was so ugly
now, and turning red.

"I'm just trying to explain, to get it
through your . . ."

"What did you call me?"

"I called you what you're acting like—
an asshole."

And suddenly he lifted his right hand
and slapped her face hard.

Claire brought her own hand to her
cheek. She rubbed the spot where he'd
struck her. When she looked at Hank, *he*
looked hurt, as if *he* had been the one
who'd been assaulted. Hank reached
out to her.

"Claire, I'm sorry. That was the weed
talking . . ."

She turned away, lowering her head,
not wanting him to see her cry.

He tried to touch her.

But Claire hurried toward the door.
Before she walked out, she turned and
spoke: "You *are* an asshole."

Chapter 3

As it turned out, Claire didn't have time to wrap ice in a dishrag and apply it to her hurt cheek. She didn't even have time for a few well-deserved tears.

That's because the phone rang. One of her sisters about Mom? Lizzie, probably. Definitely not Emily calling from New York. Her lawyer sister was probably toiling away in her office, even on the weekend.

"Claire Donoghue?" the voice on the other end asked. Not Lizzie.

"Yes, but whatever you're selling, we

don't need it. Sorry. I know you're just trying to make a living."

"This is Officer Louise Gastineau of the Myrtle Beach Police Department. Are you the mother of August Donoghue?"

Gus! Their fourteen-year-old was supposed to be in his bedroom, grounded for life after having been hauled in by the police for upending the portable potties left at the beach from the Halloween carnival.

"What happened? Is Gus hurt?" Claire asked.

"No," said the officer. "He's feeling just fine. In fact, he may be feeling *too* fine. He seems pretty stoned. So stoned that he's sleeping on the floor in the mall. Right outside the Hollister store. Near Target."

"What's going to happen to him?" Claire asked.

"Nothing much, if you can get down here and get him out of the mall. We didn't *find* any pot on him. Must have smoked every grain he had. He's just sleeping the sleep of the truly happy. Only he has an awful lot of Christmas shoppers stepping over and around him. Including one of his concerned teachers, who saw Gus and called us right away."

Claire thanked Officer Gastineau, who commiserated with her, adding that she had "three teenagers of my own." Then Claire called for the eleven-year-old twins, Toby and Gabrielle, to aid in the rescue mission. She couldn't help thinking of the classic phrase "Like father, like son." God, she hated that idea.

Claire didn't even bother telling Hank where she and the twins were headed. Just before she ripped out of the driveway, she looked up at the house and saw him at the window. He was inhaling from a substantial joint and finger-waving bye-bye to her.

She was definitely going to her mother's for Christmas, with or without Hank. To be honest, she couldn't wait to go home.

Chapter 4

The sleeping arrangements in Claire's house that night were highly creative, to say the least, but mostly sad, really sad. Hank slept on the foldout couch that he had occupied most of the day. Gus slept on the kitchen floor because Claire, Toby, and Gabrielle couldn't carry him another foot.

It worked out, in an oddball sort of way. The kitchen turned out to be a fairly convenient spot for Gus. When he awoke at three in the morning with an advanced case of the munchies, he was where a guy should be to eat an entire box of Cinnamon Toast Crunch, a half jar of peanut butter, and about a half pound of baking chocolate.

Claire was afraid that when Hank's weed wore off, he would come upstairs and try to fall asleep next to her.

So she covered herself completely with quilts and blankets and tried to fall asleep on the white wicker sofa in the sunroom.

Of course, she knew she'd never fall asleep there. And she was right. At midnight she sat up and stared out at the small sliver of cold, moonlit beach. Then Claire did what she rarely did. She cried her eyes out. Not for herself. For everybody else in the house. She had a habit of putting herself last, just the way her mother did.

The tears came rushing down her puffy, aching cheek. She finally buried her face in a quilt to keep the noise of her weeping from her sleeping family. But she just couldn't stop the cascade of tears.

Yes, she thought, I can forgive Gus. He's a teenager.

What did he do that was so awful?

Some mischief with the stupid portable toilets. Then he got stoned like a million other misguided American teenagers. But she could not forgive Hank, not anymore. Damn him. Most husbands were *not* getting stoned on Sunday afternoons that could be spent with their families; most husbands were *not* slapping their wives across the face. And if there were other husbands like that, well, Claire didn't want to be married to any of them either. So now what did she do?

Claire knew she was strong—she'd had the twins via natural childbirth (twenty-six hours of labor), still ran three miles a day—but, shoot, she thought, you can be the strongest person in the world and still make some bad decisions and have a pretty miserable life.

Her cell phone rang. What the? Oh, who else? It was her sister Lizzie, the sister who lived seven miles from Gaby up in Housatonic.

"I wake you?" Lizzie asked.

"No, I'm just sitting up reading. You know me, Lizard. Read till I drop."

"Nerd. Bookworm. I wanted to call

earlier, but Mike was feeling good enough to go out to dinner. So we all stuffed ourselves down at Bub's Barbecue."

"How's Mike doing?"

"Same. Good days and bad. Still telling jokes. He's really a trouper. I admire him."

"Well, at least you all had a little fun today. That's good. I admire *you.*"

"Yeah, thanks," Lizzie sighed. Then, with enthusiasm, she said, "Anyway, what do you think the story is with Gaby?"

"I think the story is that she's getting married. To whom—I have no idea. Maybe Tom Hayden?"

"You don't think she's telling stories?"

"Mom loves a tease, a good mystery, but no. Anyway, I think it's great."

A pause. Claire spoke again.

"I said 'I think it's great.' Don't you?"

A shorter pause.

"I guess so. I mean, yes. Yes. I think it's great."

"What's the matter, Liz? I need some backstory here."

"It's just . . . I know this is going to sound stupid. I know it's irrational . . . but it seems like . . . I don't know . . . I really miss Dad."

"I hate to say this, Liz. This is tough for me. But do you think it has something to do with the fact that Mike is pretty sick right now?"

Loudly and almost jokingly Lizzie replied, "Well, of course it does, Dr. Phil."

They both laughed like the good friends and confidantes they'd always been.

"What does Mike think about it?" Claire asked. "The wedding? The mystery groom?"

"He says there's nothing the Summerhill women can do that would surprise him. Is Hank . . . somewhat with the program?"

He doesn't have a fricking clue. "Oh, yeah. Hank's a worrywart about the weather, but he thinks it will be fun." *Staying in South Carolina and smoking weed until he drops.*

Another pause, a chance for Claire to talk her heart out, to spill about Hank the asshole. "So, you guys are good, though?" she asked her sister.

The chance to spill had passed.

"Yeah, we're good, C. Nothing an extra ten thousand a year wouldn't make better. But tomorrow I'm headed over to Mom's house. I'll get more information out of her. Mom will blab."

"Forget it. My money's on Mom," said Claire. "Gaby wants everybody home for Christmas. And you know what, she's right. We need to get together. And meet our new dad."

They said their good-byes. Claire returned to her view of the beach. Why hadn't she told Lizzie that she wanted to plunge a carving knife through Hank's heart?

Why? For the same reason Lizzie never complained about having to drive Mike to chemo twice a week or about his being struck by cancer at thirty-six. Why? Because *they* were Summerhill women. And that's the way Summerhill women had to be. Strong and tough. Claire and Lizzie and Emily and, of course, the strongest of them all, Gaby.

So who the hell are you marrying,

Mom? Why the big secret? Why all the mystery? Claire was betting on Tom Hayden. But maybe it was Jacob Coleman. Jacob was a real cutie.

Chapter 5

EMILY

Emily Summerhill, Gaby's youngest and, in many ways, most complicated daughter, had this small, muffled voice inside her head, a voice that said over and over again, *"Run, Emily, run."*

It was private code for "Succeed, Emily, succeed."

Run, Emily, run.

So Emily got into Wellesley. Emily got a 3.94 GPA. Then Emily got into Columbia Law School.

Run, Emily, run.

And Emily made *Columbia Law Review* and published the forty-page article "Medicaid Fraud: The Conundrum That Defies All Former Legal Precedents." Alan Dershowitz sent her an e-mail calling it one of the best *Review* pieces he'd read in years.

Run, Emily, run.

And Emily became a senior associate at Dale, Hardy, Dunwoodie, a law firm responsible for defending major British oil companies against stringent American environmental regulations that weren't consistently or uniformly enforced.

Run, Emily, run.

And she was certain that this was the year she would be made partner. She was only twenty-nine years old. Partner before thirty was practically unheard of. But Emily felt she was perfectly capable of achieving the unheard-of.

So at precisely 5 a.m., she was on the 6 train hurtling down Lexington Avenue to the Financial District. At five thirty-five, fortified with only a no-foam skim latte, she was at her desk.

Oh, it was early, all right.

But when you worked at Dale, Hardy, one of the toughest law firms in New York, you had to play it tough and fierce yourself. As her first boss had told her, "If you don't play tough here, we won't just chew you up and spit you out. We'll chew you up and then we'll *shit* you out." And that was from one of the nicer bosses, a woman.

Emily took a gulp of her latte, then checked her BlackBerry for the e-mails she had missed during the subway ride downtown.

One in particular jumped out.

Emily, sweets,
   I'm assuming your silence since my last video means you're swamped with work. So I assume that you're deliriously happy about my marriage news. I'll also assume that you and Bart will be coming up with sleigh bells on for Christmas. You wouldn't let your mom down and miss her wedding? See you and Dr. Bart on Christmas, when all will be revealed. I love you. Both of you!

Well, Mom was right about one thing: Emily *was* definitely swamped. The fact that she billed six hundred dollars per hour for that swamping made it feel more overwhelming, not less. In the next few days her team was trying to land a huge oil monopoly in Edinburgh. She was personally researching a British Petroleum violation of a New Mexican desert preserve. And, finally, she was appearing in the New York Court of Appeals in less than four hours for one of Dale, Hardy's rare pro bono cases.

She suddenly heard her mother's voice in her head reciting the Summerhill family motto: "Be a giver, not a taker." And the thing was, Emily believed in that philosophy. She just wasn't living it very well.

Emily clicked on the file labeled "Eduardo Lopez." Lopez was a forty-six-year-old father of four. He was accused of raping a woman in an elevator in the Sara Roosevelt housing project. He'd been convicted and had already served four years in prison. Now, even though there was new DNA evidence, supplied by the Innocence Project, that could probably exonerate him, the state prosecutors were fighting it. Why was that?

Because it would embarrass the hell out of their department.

As for fighting? The attorney general's office had no idea . . . Wait until they met Emily Summerhill in court.

Run, Emily, run.

Chapter 6

"I am living with human pigs, Señora Summerhill. And murderers. I miss my kids like the sunlight," Eduardo Lopez told Emily as they held their brief visit in a hallway outside Judge Geraldine De-Resta's courtroom down at 100 Centre Street in Manhattan.

Eduardo, a small, frail man to begin with, seemed smaller and frailer than ever to Emily. The orange jumpsuit he wore made him look like an airless balloon. Three correctional police guarded him, as if this tiny would-be criminal had a shot at escaping, or harming Emily, which made no sense at all.

When they entered the courtroom, Judge DeResta was already seated. Emily knew her as a brusque, no-nonsense sort.

She also knew Assistant District Attorney Michael Petrillo as a fast-talking, street-smart attorney, almost as tenacious as Emily herself. Petrillo's case was blatantly unjust and unfair, but sometimes that didn't make a difference in a Manhattan courtroom.

"I'd like to make this as brief as possible," Judge DeResta began. "Mr. Lopez is here on court visitation from Sullivan Correctional. Defense counsel claims new DNA evidence to enter in appeal. Please begin, Counselor, and please be concise and to the point."

Emily, who had dressed down for this occasion in criminal court, unbuttoned her gray cardigan and adjusted her white cotton blouse.

"Your Honor, a lab facility in Stamford, Connecticut, has discovered stored DNA that was taken from a semen stain on the victim's sweat shorts at the time of the crime. At that time, technology did not allow accurate identification of DNA mixed with perspiration and urine.

"Well, that was then. Current science does allow for such testing. Dr. Arthur Conover is here from NYC Forensics to verify the validity of that statement."

Judge DeResta, who had spent the last few minutes shuffling papers, said, "I'll take your word for it, Ms. Summerhill. Go on."

Emily continued, "For almost three years we have been trying to get the lab, Human Case Genetics, to release their sample. Each time they were about to do it, the DA's office managed to get a stop-action."

Judge DeResta looked at Petrillo directly.

"Is that true, Mr. Petrillo?"

"Your Honor, we respectfully petitioned the court, and they agreed that the *State v. Lopez* case was closed and that, furthermore, Human Case Genetics was not a New York–approved facility for DNA storage."

Emily clamped her tongue between her teeth. It was a trick Gaby had taught her so that every single thought she had didn't come spilling out of her mouth.

"But Human Case Genetics was approved at the time of the alleged crime," Emily finally said.

Petrillo's face was already bright red. He'd come here to tussle, to fight dirty, to win whatever the cost.

"Not 'alleged,' Ms. Summerhill. Mr. Lopez was found guilty!"

Emily went on as if he hadn't even spoken. "Mr. Lopez has given a new sample of his DNA. Under the supervision of Dr. Conover, a comparison has been made between that sample and the sample from the victim's sweat shorts."

Judge DeResta spoke in her characteristic singsong manner.

"And they don't match."

"No, Your Honor." Emily looked over at Eduardo. His chin was down. His eyes were filled with tears. He was the embodiment of anxiety.

"Mr. Petrillo, do you agree with this conclusion?"

"No, I do not, Your Honor," Petrillo said as he stood up.

"Why am I not surprised?" Judge De-Resta said, again in that singsong manner of hers. Emily couldn't tell whether the judge was becoming angry with her, Petrillo, or both of them. Or what it would mean for her client, her innocent client.

"Your Honor, Eduardo Lopez was positively identified by the victim. Both in a mug book and a lineup. He was present at the Sara Roosevelt houses that evening, drinking and gambling . . ."

Emily interrupted. "Mr. Lopez was playing poker, yes, and he drank one beer."

"In any event," Petrillo said, "the jury found him guilty within an hour of being assigned deliberation."

"Objection. Amount of time of deliberation is irrelevant," said Emily.

"Sustained—and you can sit down, Mr. Petrillo."

Petrillo sat.

"And you can stand up, Mr. Lopez," Judge DeResta said, almost in the same breath.

Eduardo looked at Emily. He was frightened to death. Together they stood at the shoddy black plastic table. Judge DeResta shook her head wearily. She ran her right hand through her short gray hair.

"Mr. Lopez," Judge DeResta said, "on behalf of the State of New York, I want to apologize for the injustice of your fifty-one months of incarceration."

Eduardo looked confused. Emily took his hand. The judge continued.

"The evidence your attorney presented today exonerates you of this crime. Prosecution counsel has introduced a note of skepticism that is both unreasonable and unjustified. In fact, I'm going to discuss this matter with my clerk, because it actually could be an illegal interference with judicial protocol."

Petrillo looked down at his folded hands. He knew better than to interrupt now.

"There is little doubt in my mind," the judge went on, "that the jury would have come to a different conclusion had today's DNA testing methods been available to the court. Mr. Lopez, you are free to go."

Emily turned to him and said quietly, "You're free, Eduardo."

Eduardo wept, and his wife, in the back row, yelled *"Gracias a Dios!"* His kids ran up to hug him.

The only one happier than Eduardo was Emily. To her astonishment, she felt her hands shake and her eyes fill with tears. Eduardo embraced her, and then, it seemed, she was hugged and kissed by every aunt, uncle, niece, nephew, son, and daughter in Eduardo's family. She wanted to jump up and punch the air. And maybe include Judge DeResta in the group hug.

Until she felt a vibration in the pocket of her sweater.

Dammit.

Emily clicked on her BlackBerry. The first text message was from her boss, Daniel Wycliffe Church, "Cliff" to his friends, senior partner at her firm. She

read the message, which was short and
to the point:

Where the shit are you? We've got
real work to do here.

Run, Emily. Run.

Chapter 7

Run, run, run!

Most senior offices at the law firm of Dale, Hardy had few or no personal mementos on display—no photos of adorable children or attractive spouses, no tennis trophies, golfing plaques, or crazy-crayoned drawings with "I Love You, Daddy" on them. Nothing communicated the fact that these people had private lives, probably because they didn't.

Cliff Church did things a little differently. On his desk was a large mahogany-framed photo of a stunning blond wife and three equally photogenic blond sons. Cliff also had framed photographs of himself salmon fishing in Vancouver, fly-fishing in Idaho, surf fishing in Bali.

There was no image of him posing with a United States president, but there was a photo of Cliff and his wife at a restaurant table in Los Angeles with Reese Witherspoon and Jake Gyllenhaal. Cliff was smiling with satisfaction. The other three were roaring with laughter. What a hilarious joke Cliff must have told.

"Listen, I don't mean to knock your pro bono shit," Cliff was saying. "It's great PR and terrific chicken soup for the soul. But you and I should be reading every fucking thing about those Jap automakers we're having dinner with tonight."

Emily sank farther down into the ridiculously soft cushions on Cliff's sofa. She was pretty sure that Cliff had selected those cushions because they gave him the chance to study the legs of every woman who sat there, including herself.

Emily responded with unconcealed irritation. "I have already read every fucking thing about those . . . those gentlemen from Nissan we're having dinner with tonight. And I've read it all three times."

"Then I guess we'll be in fine shape," Cliff said. His smile was seductive. "Oh, and don't worry. I won't use words like 'Japs' or 'fucking' tonight. As you know, I can turn my political-correctness button on in a second."

"Yes," she said. "I know you can do that. You went to Andover and Harvard."

"I'll swing by your place about seven. It'll give us plenty of time to get to the restaurant. Did your gal make a rez at Momofuku like I suggested?" Cliff asked.

"No. I thought about it, and I figured we shouldn't try to out-Japanese the Japanese. We're going to Smith and Wollensky—oysters, thick steaks, and plenty of scotch."

"You are one smart lady," he said. "All wise-guy cynicism aside, I mean that, Em."

"Yes, I am," Emily said, anxious to get out of Cliff's office.

She was angry about two things. First, Cliff's sexist attitude. And second, the fact that she found him attractive. Gaby would have been so, so disappointed.

Which reminded her—*what kind of man had won Gaby's heart?*

Chapter 8

Emily, as was often the case, turned out to be right. Smith & Wollensky was an excellent choice for the men from Nissan and their potential lawyers.

"So happy not to eat sushi and sushi and sushi. Excellent beef is delicious alternative," one of the prospective clients said as she and Cliff helped three of them into a waiting London TownCar.

"Well, we're happy you enjoyed it. We did too," Emily said. "I'm also happy that Cliff-san decided to take you to a steakhouse." She distinctly heard Cliff whisper, *"Asshole."*

"We will be in contact tomorrow," said the same Japanese gentleman, and then, as Emily bowed from the neck and Cliff waved, the car took off.

"We got it!" Cliff shouted. "We fucking got it!"

"You really think so?" Emily said. As always, she was amazed by her boss's confidence and swagger. In a way, it was impressive.

"I *know* we did," Cliff said. "When you started in on the environmental restrictions for carbon compounds versus full-electric cars, they thought you were the senior senator from Michigan. For a minute there, so did I."

"I read the material three times," she said, and could feel herself blush.

She noticed that she and Cliff were walking east on Forty-ninth Street, toward the United Nations building. Not good.

"Let's stop at the Beekman Hotel. Celebration drink," he said.

"Let's wait till we get the business, Cliff."

"We've got it. C'mon. Don't jinx us, Em. One drink. Call it a pre-celebration."

"Maybe you've forgotten. I have an apartment, here in the city. I have a husband. I've got a life beyond Dale, Hardy."

He stopped walking. So Emily stopped too.

"No, you don't," he said with a grin. "You absolutely do not."

"What are you talking about, Cliff?"

"You don't have another life. Dale, Hardy is your life. The firm is your husband. The firm is your life. You spend eighty percent of your time there. You work like an animal. You don't have another life, Emily."

She didn't contradict him. His facts were at least partially correct. She didn't even engage in a discussion.

"Cliff, I'm getting a cab uptown on First Avenue," she said. She began to walk away.

"Emily!" he called out. "Hold on! Please, wait."

She froze in place, but she didn't turn. Cliff was making her nervous now.

Suddenly his arms were around her shoulders. He bent forward and nuzzled her neck. Then he kissed her cheek, and the side of her mouth.

"I'm getting a cab," Emily said. But she didn't move.

"Let's get that drink first," he said. "The Beekman's only a block or so away."

"I've got to get going."

He kissed her on the neck again. For a moment Emily thought: *If you don't respond, if you don't acknowledge it, if you don't move, then it really didn't happen. Right?* Then she thought, *No. Not right at all. This is definitely happening. Now what do I do about it?*

"You're over the line, Cliff. There's a cab over there," she said, and then moved quickly toward First Avenue.

Run, Emily. Run.

Chapter 9

GABY'S SECOND VIDEO, PART ONE

Now, this is a first! Never before have I sent a video that got three of the four of you to call me the day you received it. I should get married more often. *And, oh, yes, I assume that after you called me, you called each other. I love that.*

Okay. It's very early up here in western Mass. All you can see through the den window is darkness. That's because it's four-fifteen in the morning.

You see, I've been up all night.

Thinking.

Now here goes.

I've been thinking about your dad.

And . . . well, that's what I want to talk to you about.

Even after three years, it's as if, if we don't talk about Peter, then he's not really dead. He's just gone away for a while. You know what I mean?

Let me tell you a secret I haven't shared with anybody else. I still reach for him in the middle of the night.

And I sometimes buy lamb chops because they were Peter's favorite.

Something will happen during the day, say, in my classroom, and I'll think, oh, I can't wait to tell Peter and the kids. I know, I'm a sap. The last of the sentimentalists.

I mostly remember good times. Who wants to remember missed mortgage payments and arguments, when there are so many sweet, funny things that we shared?

You know, I just finished reading *Freedom,* and I do believe Jonathan Franzen writes beautifully, but I think he only has a partial view of what it's like to live as most of us do. He seems to think that people are empty-headed if they don't obsess about the obvious absurdities of life and that intelligent people can't possibly be happy. Well, I don't believe that's necessarily true. I think that most people can lead very satisfying lives, as long as they don't spend too much time staring at their belly buttons and worrying about things that aren't within their control.

Anyhow, I was being sentimental before I interrupted myself . . . I remember a time when Peter and I fell asleep on the dunes in Truro. Two hours later we had so much poison ivy we could barely sit in the car to drive back to the inn. But still, I treasure that lost weekend.

And I remember how proud he was of the new window he installed in Lizzie and Claire's room. Only he put it in sideways, and even today, every time I open it, I laugh. Except for today.

And when he asked me to marry him—quite beautifully, poetically—and I smiled and said "Sure," I think he was hurt a little. So then I spent at least fifteen minutes telling him all the things that I loved about him. I could do the same thing right now.

As I'm sure is the case for you guys,

not a day goes by that I don't think how unfair it was that he was taken from us. How stupid, really.

Oh, damn, I was afraid this might happen. A waterfall is coming.

Hold on. I'll be right back. I need to tell you something important.

Chapter 10

GABY'S SECOND VIDEO, PART TWO

Sorry about that. I'm okay now. You know me. Strong like bull, cry at the drop of a handkerchief.

Anyway . . . so this guy, this wonderful guy, your dad, who did everything to take care of himself. All that low-fat yogurt, organic fruit and veggies. Weighed himself every morning . . . Ran four miles every day. And then, the genetic heart-attack time bomb goes off. It was such a ridiculously short time we had with him—as a husband, as a dad, as a friend, as a soul mate.

But, you know what, one wonderful

weekend with your father was worth more than a lifetime with some other men.

So you're probably thinking, *Well, hey, if you loved Dad so much, why replace him?* I guess the point is, I can't ever "replace" him. It's just that . . . I want to be loved again.

And I really need to do something for myself. I've spent my whole life taking care of other people—no regrets—but now I'm doing something for me. Yay.

That's what you're all going to find out about this Christmas.

Don't worry. I know who the person is. I've known for some time. However, the person doesn't know who the person is. Like I said, I'm doing something for myself, and this is the way I'd like it to be.

Ohhh. And by the way, I want to remind you that there are a number of eligible and exceptional candidates around Stockbridge.

Like, well, your uncle Martin. I know you think of him as your father's kid brother, but he's only ten months younger—big deal. And I'll tell you this.

I have always had a little crush on Marty, and he's had a crush on me.

Marty is terrific. Negative side? He plays the rhythm guitar—badly. Positive side? Former wife totally out of the picture and living in California. Attractive salt-and-pepper hair, and lots of it. Very good Italian cook. Cute butt from swimming every day. Everybody's favorite house builder around here.

Oh, yes, I forgot to mention—Marty has asked to marry me.

Which doesn't mean that I said yes, does it?

Another thing that I forgot to mention, and this is a mindblower: *Marty isn't the only one who's asked.*

There are three—so far, anyway. Does that seem incredible, even unbelievable, to you? It sure does to me. Even now it does. I'm still in shock and a little numb about the whole thing.

I'll tell you how it happened. A few of us were sitting around after one of our breakfasts for the homeless in the barn. Marty, Jacob, Tom, Stacey Lee, and me.

Suddenly Marty told everybody that he'd asked me to marry him and was waiting for an answer. "You know Gaby. She does things in her own way, and according to her own clock," he said.

What happened next started as a lark, almost a skit. That's what I thought at first, anyway.

Jacob got down on one knee and—he asked if I would marry him. "I'm serious, Gaby. I'm a serious person when I have to be," he said. "I'm asking you to marry me. I think I've been in love with you for the last couple of years. I'll be a very good husband, Gaby."

The way Jacob asked was so beautiful and thoughtful, it was hard to imagine he hadn't composed and rehearsed it before that morning.

Then Tom got up and stood right in front of me. My God, what was going on? He was the most intense of all—but Tom is always intense—and his face was red when he confessed that he'd probably been in love with me for twenty years—but he said it in the sweetest way imaginable. He's always been confident in athletics but a little shy in some social situations.

"I can't let you go to Marty or Jacob

without at least telling you how I feel. I adore you, Gaby. I just didn't know if you were ready yet. If you are . . . will you marry me? Will you at least think about it?"

I was stunned, flabbergasted, speechless, and I finally said that, well, I would have to get back to them. I didn't know what else I could possibly say.

They were all so sincere, and I care deeply about each of them. I couldn't hurt anybody's feelings, and I wasn't even sure how I felt at that moment. It all happened so fast and was so unexpected.

But now I know what I want—*whom* I want. I don't think I've ever been surer of anything in my life. I am utterly in love with the person I want to spend the rest of my life with.

Okay, look. Enough jibber-jabbering about me. I've got a few chores to do around here.

So there's just one thing left to say: See you at Christmas, and see you in my dreams. I love you all so much.

Chapter 11

Gaby decided she would make the DVD dupes later, then take them to the FedEx store. Right now, she had to get out to the barn. Her workday had officially begun.

She stopped for half a second to check herself in the hall mirror. "Not too bad," she said, "for being up half the night."

She was going to the barn to feed breakfast to twenty or more homeless folks from town. She'd been doing it every day for over twenty years. Her parents and grandparents had done it before her—made breakfast for migrant workers who came in the autumn to pick apples and pumpkins, and for families overwhelmed by the Great Depression, then for unemployed workers from the glove and hat and shoe factories across the border in upstate New York.

One of the best parts was doing these breakfasts with her friends, her buds, male and female. What made it even more enticing these days: Three of them had asked for Gaby's hand in marriage. She hadn't said yes, but she hadn't said no either. And none of them had taken back his offer. In fact, they were all pressing her for an answer. There had even been an argument or two between them.

Tom Hayden owned a local farm. He was a former professional hockey player, handsome as sin. And possibly the sweetest man around. Jacob Coleman, the rabbi at Am Shalom Temple in Great Barrington, was another do-gooder like Gaby. He was a serious man, but with a terrific sense of humor. No one could make her laugh like he did. Marty Summerhill was Peter's younger brother. Her pal for years. Always, *always* there for Gaby. The fourth friend present was Stacey Lee Pashcow, a middle-aged divorcée whom Gaby had grown up with. Hardly a day passed that she and Stacey Lee didn't have lunch or coffee together, and a couple of times a month they'd go to Boston to hear the symphony or maybe a Dave Matthews concert. Once or twice a week Gaby stopped by Stacey Lee's restaurant/store, the Farmer's Wife, in Stockbridge, where she helped out—chopping chicken breasts, fluting pie crusts, icing the county-famous Chocolate Tart Stacey Lee.

This morning her latest video performance had made Gaby late, so she jogged toward the cooking area in the barn. What was it that Emily always said—*Run, Emily, run?*

"*Hate* those powdered eggs," she said to Jacob, who was stirring a pot of yellow goop on the wood-stove in the corner.

The good-looking rabbi leaned in and kissed her cheek. "I know you do, purist that you are. But until those ten hens of yours can produce forty eggs a day, this is the best we can do. Maybe a nice Christian miracle would help? Can you arrange that?"

Gaby patted Jacob's shoulder and smiled at Marty, who was about to pass out silverware and napkins to the hungry-looking people sitting around three wooden tables.

Then Gaby spotted Stacey Lee, who was practically whirling around the barn—sweeping up goat manure, consolidating trash from yesterday's breakfast, doing the lousy jobs that no one else wanted to do.

Finally Gaby joined Tom, dishing hot oatmeal into bowls. She worked quickly and efficiently at his side, noticing that almost every bowl had a chip in it. She insisted that they use real dinnerware—no paper or plastic, except for the napkins.

"Morning, Tom, you look terrific this a.m."

"Morning, Gaby, you're gorgeous as always. God, *just look at you!*"

Gaby grinned. "And they wonder why I work the oatmeal bar with you."

Tom smiled back at her. "You could make it official. You and me? Oatmeal forever?" Of course Gaby didn't answer.

At that point, Stacey Lee began collecting money at the tables. Gaby felt that everybody should pay something for breakfast, even if it was just a few pennies, and even if they had to borrow the small change from her or one of the other helpers.

"Thanks for coming!" Gaby announced, as she did every morning. "We couldn't do this without you. Now, who's hungry?"

Chapter 12

SETH AND ANDIE

Gaby's only son, Seth, was singing *before* breakfast that morning:

**Hark the herald angels sing
Gaby Summerhill is marrying.
Folks will come from far and
  near.
Seth and Andie will be there.
We're coming. We're coming.**

"Are you loving this dumb song like I'm loving it?" Seth said to Andie.
Andie just smiled.
They were sitting on a lumpy green

sofa that she'd tried to spruce up with orange plastic pillows from a dollar store in Chinatown. But Boston didn't have a very big Chinatown, and Boston's Chinatown didn't have very exciting pillows for a buck. And obviously, Seth and Andie didn't have a lot of spare bucks for decorating, or much of anything else.

"I know the song you want," Seth said. Then his fingers attacked the three-octave keyboard on his lap as he sang:

Wedding bell, wedding bell,
Wedding bell rock!
Gaby's a bride, oh, my, what a
**   shock!**

Now Andie smiled again, and this smile was wide, toothy, totally irresistible. Whenever Seth told her that, she answered, "I've spent my whole life saving my smile for someone like you." And Seth knew that was the truth. Andie's parents had died in an auto accident when she was twelve. She recalled her teenage years as a wasteland of loneliness—not bad, not cruel, just achingly lonely. So when she met Seth, and when it was clear that he loved her, she decided to enfold him with all the caring and love she'd been keeping inside since her parents' death.

"C'mon," he said. "You like 'Wedding Bell Rock' better."

"It's not that I like it *better,* Seth. It's just that I think it *works* better with my visual."

She held up her sketch—a charming, funny, and irreverent cartoon of Gaby and ten unidentifiable men disguised by ski caps and scarves, all riding in an open sleigh.

Right behind them in a wacky convertible was a couple—obviously Seth and Andie—chasing after them like the Keystone Kops.

Seth slid the keyboard off his lap. Then he leaned over and kissed her.

"We'll go with 'Wedding Bell Rock.' That's the best."

"You are the nicest boyfriend," she said, and she kissed him again. This time the kiss lasted longer. "And the best roommate ever."

"Should we finish up the song and the card or should we . . . you know," he asked, "before we have to go to work?"

Andie slid over on top of him. "You know?"

"You know," he said. "It's good we sit around in our underwear sometimes. That way we're ready to seize the moment. Among other things."

"You remember what your mother said—that time she paid a surprise visit in the middle of the afternoon?"

"'You two always walk around like you're in a French movie'?"

Gaby had also told them she thought it was adorable. *They* were adorable— both so slim and tall, and obviously head over heels in love with each other.

But Seth hadn't told Gaby what was on their minds lately. They were a big bundle of nerves and anxiety, actually. Because—

The prestigious New York publishing house Alfred A. Knopf was considering Seth's novel *The Dream Chasers.* The book had been passed around for six weeks, and now Seth checked his e-mail about every fifteen minutes. He was getting as jumpy as his sister Emily, the lawyer in New York.

But he still hadn't heard from Knopf. So that meant he was still the most overqualified receptionist at Arnold Worldwide, a Boston ad agency at Center Plaza.

Meanwhile, a few floors and offices away at Little, Brown, Andie was busy doing illustrations for children's books. "Toddler books, not teens or tweens or chapter books," she would say, using the lingo of the trade. "I am the perfect visual communicator with the under-three crowd."

"So, what's it going to be?" Seth said, gently rubbing the sides of her arms and hips and legs.

"We should get this card done," she said as she kissed him. "Gaby's a bride, oh, my, what a shock!"

Chapter 13

At eight twenty-nine that morning, Seth, still a bundle of nerves and unfulfilled expectations, swiped his ID card through the elevator turnstile at Arnold Worldwide. He sat down at his desk and booted up his computer. Doctoral candidate in American lit and promising novelist that he was, he would spend the rest of the day greeting visitors and saying, "I'll buzz back and let him know you're here."

His first order of business was to scan his e-mail and see if the Almighty Knopf had gotten in touch with him in the forty minutes since he'd checked his e-mail at home.

Nope, nothing from them.

Just the first of many e-mails from Andie. "It's been a half hour and I miss you already. Just kidding, kind of. The people at Knopf probably aren't even in their offices yet."

So Seth hung his old cowboy jacket in the closet. Then he arranged the magazines in order—*AdAge* and *Ad-Week* and *Creativity* fanned out in one pile, *Wired, Face,* and *L'Uomo Vogue* in another. He checked to make certain the night supply supervisor had stacked more paper cups in the cubbyhole with the water cooler (they called it a bubbler in Boston). Then he thought about how his BA in Renaissance literature at Dartmouth had prepared him for this job. He truly was a man for all seasons.

At eight forty-five the agency account executives came marching in—not bad people, but with a sense of self-importance in their "How you doing, Seth, my man?" or, skipping the niceties, "I'm expecting the ad manager from J and J at nine. Just send him back. Make him feel like he belongs here. You know how to do it, Seth."

The creative types wouldn't start appearing until close to nine-thirty, some of them even later, some not at all. "I'm crashing at home today, Seth. Cover for me." Seth retrieved the newspapers from outside the elevators and placed them on the coffee table. The *Boston Globe,* the *Wall Street Journal, USA Today,* the *New York Times.* The day was ready to begin.

He removed the lid from his Dunkin' Donuts coffee and refreshed his personal e-mail page.

And there it was! The e-mail he'd been waiting for for weeks, the e-mail from the editor who'd first read and loved his novel at Knopf. Well, she *was* in early after all.

Hi, Seth.
I'll get right to what you want to know. Unfortunately, the news is not good. At yesterday's editorial meeting the committee decided to pass on *The Dream Chasers.* The

feeling is that in this tough economic climate a first novel with a coming-of-age theme in a science fiction framework is too challenging for the average reader, even the literary reader that Knopf cultivates and treasures.

Everyone agreed—even Sonny Mehta—that your novel is strongly realized and a uniquely written and well-constructed piece. But I am certain those observations do little to assuage your disappointment in this outcome.

I know there is a very good publisher out there who will jump at the chance to take on this fine project. And we at Knopf look forward to seeing your future work.

I will call you in a few weeks, to see if you're starting another project. And, Seth, please know that I share your disappointment in not moving forward with *Dream Chasers.*

Best always,
Mariana Gortensen, Editor

Hell, no, you don't share my disappointment, Mariana. Not even close. But hell, yes, you're right about something else: This does little to assuage my disappointment in this outcome!

Seth couldn't help reading the e-mail a few more times. Once he committed it to memory he did the only thing that might calm him down and bring him a little peace.

He called Gaby. He got her in the classroom, and she still spent several minutes talking him down off the ledge. She told him that he was a very good writer—and she knew what made a good writer—that she loved him enormously, and that now he had to suck it up.

For some reason that helped Seth a lot.

Suck it up. That was his mom.

Chapter 14

"It stinks. No, it's even worse than that," said Gaby to Seth. She had taken her cell phone outside her classroom. She knew that this was a call she needed to take, and that she mustn't cut poor Seth short. She believed in always treating her children with sympathy when they had a problem, but never lying to them. She wasn't about to feed Seth some fantasy like "Oh, someone else will buy your novel" or "Just think of it as a bad bump along the road to a Pulitzer."

"Yeah, it sucks," he said. "It's just that Mariana was so enthusiastic. Everybody

was loving it, she was saying. Everybody . . . everybody was. Oh, what difference does it make?"

"Well, wait. It does make a difference,
Seth. The editor liked it. Other people at
Knopf liked it. She recommended they
buy it. Other people agreed. It just got
screwed up somehow. So let's not give
up hope immediately. Of course, I'll
never buy another book from Knopf."

"Hold on a second, Mom," he said.
And then Gaby heard Seth say, "Go
right on back, sir. He's expecting you.
You know where it is, fourth office on
the left." A pause. Then, "Mom? You still
there?"

"Seth, don't get blinded by your disappointment. Be disappointed. Cry a little. Yell a little. Drink a few martinis.
Then suck it up."

"I know, but it's hard, Mom. I had so
much hope riding on this one. How
dumb," he said, and Gaby thought she
could her son's voice cracking. She remembered what her own mother used
to say: "A mother is only as happy as
her unhappiest child." She felt as if poor

Seth were lying on his shield in front of her.

"I've got to go. I've got an important receptionist's job to do. And I will suck it up."

"I love you, more than I love the goats, and you know how I feel about those goats," Gaby said. "Remember, you're my favorite son."

"Mom. I'm your *only* son."

They both laughed a small laugh, then said goodbye.

Seth glanced at the e-mail from Knopf one more time. Then he pressed the delete button. He would never buy a Knopf book again either.

Chapter 15

GABY'S THIRD VIDEO

It's time that I talked about and sang the praises of some wonderful men. They're all willing to go along with this great mystery of mine, and have agreed that it's time that Gaby did something for herself. At least that's what they're saying to my face. I've never cared much what people say behind my back.

You all know Jacob—whom I happen to know Claire has had a crush on since she was twelve or thirteen years old. At first I thought she wanted to convert to Judaism so she could have a bat mitzvah and get cool gifts like her friend

Lauren. Then one day when she said, "Rabbi Jacob was jogging past our house this morning . . . and he looked so adorable in his running shorts," I knew it wasn't just about bat mitzvah gifts.

And, Claire, don't bother to e-mail everyone and say it's not true. I know it is . . . because he did look adorable in his running shorts. Jacob *still* looks adorable, better than ever. He's also smart and sensitive and sensible. He's also funny. I was standing with him at the Silverman wedding a couple weeks back when a woman, who shall remain nameless on these very public tapes, walked up and complained, "Rabbi, they're serving shrimp." Jacob nodded thoughtfully and said, "Hmm. Let's hope they don't enjoy it very much."

Then there's Tom Hayden, the *Massachusetts* Tom Hayden.

We'll just ignore the fact that I once heard Tom say he'd rather "hang by my toes for a month" than ever get married again. But we won't ignore the fact that he bears more than a passing resemblance to Brett Favre, whom, honestly, I used to admire more for his Wrangler commercials than his football-playing abilities. He *was* football—right? (Or wait, should that be *is*—maybe he's un-retired again?) Anyway, Tom Hayden. He teaches all the local kids not just how to play hockey, but how to love playing hockey. Tom also loves funny movies, and so do I. He takes me hiking and even canoeing. Did I mention that Tom is funny too? He must have a sense of humor to get into a canoe with me.

Hold on a sec. I've got company— maybe it's Tom? Maybe his ears were burning? Maybe he wants to propose a second time?

Chapter 16

"Aha! Caught you! Making a porno flick, I bet! Did I hear Tom's name? Is he here? Is Tom Hayden the one, Gaby? *Tom, are you in there?* Is this a Restoration comedy? One of those amusing farces?"

"You scared the hell out of me, Stacey Lee," Gaby said as she put away the video equipment in the corner of the den. "Will you ever learn to ring the doorbell?"

"Doorbell? I figure I'm like family. Even closer than family," Stacey Lee said. She and Gaby shared a hug. "You know, you should be sending me one of those family message DVDs." She whispered in Gaby's ear. "*Who is it, Gaby? This is driving me crazy. I've been your best friend since first grade. Isn't that worth anything?*"

"Give it up, Stacey Lee. Come on, it's time for our meeting in the barn," Gaby said.

"I know that, sweetie. But let me ask you one more time: Do you really think it's a good idea to have a wedding-planning meeting with so many people? Some of whom have *proposed* to you?"

"It's six people, Stacey Lee. Just the volunteers from the Barn Breakfast group. You. Me. And the boys."

"The problem remains—no one knows who you're marrying."

"That's not true," said Gaby. "*I* know. And the others have agreed to let this play out the way I want it to, the way I *need* it to. They want all the kids home for Christmas too. And they respect my wishes, my style. Always have. That's part of the package with me."

Stacey Lee threw her arms up in the air. It was clear to Gaby that she was actually enjoying the drama too. She just wanted to read the last page of the mystery before anyone else did.

"Everyone will find out Christmas Day. My family. My friends. The goats and the hens. Meanwhile we have to plan a wedding party."

"Have you got an extra sweater? It's suddenly gotten so cold. It actually feels like snow," Stacey Lee said.

"Oh, toughen up. I'll keep you warm," Gaby said, putting her arm around Stacey Lee. Together they walked out to the barn. Gaby said not another word about the suitors and, out of respect and love, neither did Stacey Lee.

Chapter 17

"Ah, the beautiful bride and the equally beautiful matron of honor," Tom said as Gaby and Stacey Lee sauntered into the barn. For an ex–hockey player, he had a nice way with words.

"You mean the attractive but matronly matron of honor," Stacey Lee said.

"If every woman looked like you, no one would mind growing a day older," said Marty. He was competing with Tom, or at least messing with his head.

"You always were my favorite Summerhill," Stacey Lee said and grinned. Everyone in the room had been friends for years. Decades, in some cases. Not only did they put up with Gaby, she was the flame they fluttered around like moths.

The men in question were seated at one of the rustic wood tables. Gaby and Stacey Lee joined them.

"I have exactly one hour before I have to teach a Hebrew class," said Jacob. "I don't particularly like this group of kids. If it's possible, they're even more self-involved than their parents. But I have to teach them as if they were my own children, of course."

"And I'm on O.B. call," said Kurt Henley the veterinarian, who was just about the only man in town who hadn't asked for Gaby's hand in marriage. "Diabetic sow about to give birth." Kurt took his cell phone from his pocket and put it on the table. "In case she calls."

Gaby looked at them all for a moment. Not only was this a group of very good men, it was a group of very good-*looking* men.

Tom was in faded jeans, a long-sleeved gray Henley (he always said "It's just my winter undershirt"), a bright green-and-yellow flannel shirt. A few days of blond stubble topped off the look.

Then there was her brother-in-law, Marty. Gaby always saw the tiniest trace of Peter in Marty's face. They were clearly brothers. Peter had been older and thinner and shorter, but not *that much* older and thinner and shorter. Then there was the voice. That New England *r*—a sound that always came out as *ah.*

And finally, Jacob. Her sweet, kind, mildly neurotic Jacob. He had his black suit on, a wrinkled white shirt with the top button open. Very hip, actually, very downtown Boston or New York. His jacket collar was casually flipped up on his neck, his beard trimmed neatly with just that little tuft under the lower lip.

"Well, I do appreciate you all taking the time to stop by. That a man would leave the side of a pregnant pig to help plan my wedding truly touches me," Gaby said to Kurt, and she put her hand to her heart.

"You know," said Kurt with a grin,

"I've been thinking, Gaby, of maybe asking you—"

"Don't you dare!" Gaby said with a laugh.

"Right, right. My wife would probably object . . . Maybe not."

"So," Gaby continued, "it's Christmas and it's a wedding, on the same day. I've already thought of all the predictable ideas, and I've already rejected them. That means *no* wedding cake in the shape of a Christmas tree. And definitely *no* Mr. and Mrs. Santa Claus on top of the cake."

Silence.

Tom, Marty, and Jacob looked straight ahead. Then they looked down at the old table. Then they looked at one another. They looked everywhere but at Gaby.

"Ideas?" Stacey Lee said.

"Oh, for God's sake," Tom said. "This is nuts, Gaby."

"My getting married is nuts?" asked Gaby with a tilt of her head.

"No. It's *great* that you're getting married," Marty broke in. He got to his feet, pushed back his chair, and knocked it over in the process.

"Though it would be nice if you told us *who* you were marrying," Jacob said.

"Yeah, that would be a good twist," added Marty. "Surprise everybody in the middle of the story."

"But that's not what we're talking about," said Jacob. "Why would you get the three of us here to help you plan a wedding?"

Gaby stood up. "Why? I can give you the answer to that one. Because you're my friends. All of you—and Stacey Lee—are my buddies. I know that's a little unusual. But that's the way it happened, and I don't know about you, but I love it. Like that saying—I love you guys!"

"We love you, Gaby!" they all said, pretty much in unison. "And Stacey Lee too."

"Otherwise, we wouldn't put up with this goofy shit," said Marty with a grin.

"Not for a minute!" said Jacob.

The laughter continued, and Gaby went to the refrigerator and removed two bottles of Dom Pérignon champagne. She filled plastic glasses with the good stuff, and then they all held their glasses high.

"To our beloved bride," Marty shouted, "and God knows, she is beloved."

"And to my friends," Gaby said, "the best friends anywhere."

"And to our groom," Stacey Lee said. "Whoever the hell that might be."

Chapter 18

LIZZIE, MIKE, AND TALLULAH

First came Mike's headaches. Lizzie had said, "Oh, Mike, it's probably just one of your sinus infections." A week later, when the headaches hadn't stopped, she told him that his store, Housatonic Hardware and Bait, could do without him for two hours while he went to see the doctor.

Mike put off making a doctor's appointment, of course. He stopped complaining too. Then one night while he was changing a ceiling bulb in the kitchen he got dizzy and fell off a stepladder.

A week later, Mike reported, "Dr. Sassoon says my ears are fine. Says my pressure is on the low side. Maybe that's why I'm getting the dizzy spells. He wants me to go to Pittsfield and get an RMI."

Lizzie corrected him. "MRI," she said. "It's not an RMI, Mike. It's called an MRI."

Mike didn't say anything more. He smiled at her. She smiled back. It was, she knew (and she didn't know how she knew), the beginning of his memory confusion. Three days later Mike was diagnosed with a benign meningioma.

Benign. That was the word Lizzie hung on to. Benign, she thought. "Benign" means good. "Benign" means Mike will be okay. Even though the neurologist said, "It can grow. It can grow and it can choke the brain."

Lizzie and Mike—and Gaby—began learning the language of brain cancer. Primary tumor, electron microscopy, hyperfractionated radiation therapy, anaplastic astrocytoma. They searched every website—medical, homeopathic, spiritual. They read the stories of others, focusing on the tales of survivors like the "miracle girl" from Austin, Texas, who stunned doctors as her tumor miraculously grew smaller. Gaby was there every step of the way, but she never interfered, never offered an opinion unless it was asked for.

Lizzie and Mike talked with Emily's husband in New York, a neurological resident. Bart belonged to the generation that always insisted on the truth. "It could be a bad result," Bart said. "It's not a foregone conclusion, but the news is not great."

When they hung up the phone Mike said, "What the hell does Bart know? He's a kid—like Emily. He's not even a real doctor yet." Lizzie pretended to agree, but she knew that, like her sister Emily, Bart was a superstar. He knew plenty.

A few days later Lizzie noticed that the left side of Mike's face had begun drooping—ever so slightly, but she noticed it all the same. So did Tallulah.

To Mike and Lizzie's relief, and to nobody's surprise, Gaby had put herself in charge of eight-year-old Tallulah. The grandmother and granddaughter had sleepovers and hikes with Tom through the Berkshires and visits to Kurt's farm. They took a candy-making course with Stacey Lee Saturday mornings at the culinary school in Springfield. And Uncle Marty came to visit at least every other day.

It was Gaby whom Tallulah decided to ask the question they all knew she would eventually ask: "Is my daddy going to die?" Gaby closed her eyes for a moment, and she thought about what she would want to know if she were an eight-year-old with a very sick dad. She'd want the truth. So Gaby gave her the truth, gently: "I don't think he's going to die. The doctors don't think he's going to die. But, sweetie, we can't be sure yet. I won't lie to you. We'll just pray for the best, and we'll wait and see. I'll be right here with you."

It was never hard for Gaby to tell the truth. But this time she hated every word that came out of her mouth. And later that night, as they ate too many of the chocolate-covered cherries they'd made that morning, Gaby and Tallulah held each other, and they both cried.

"You're a brave, brave girl, Tula," Gaby told her.

"I know," said the little girl. "I got it from you."

Chapter 19

Two days after the diagnosis Mike had surgery at Mass. General in Boston. The operation was performed by Dr. Raj Soorgan, "a very big man" in neurosurgery whom Bart vouched for. Mike and Lizzie found some comfort in knowing he was a very big man, but they were smart enough to know that patients were always being operated on by very big men. And what difference did it make when there were so many very dead patients?

Mike spent nine hours that morning

and afternoon on the table, under the knife.

When Dr. Soorgan came out to the family waiting room to speak to Lizzie and Gaby—and Emily, who had taken two days off from work to be there with her sister—he spoke carefully, as if his words were being recorded, which they were.

"He came through it fine. He's in ICU. He's responding well. And I think I got it all."

Emily clicked on her mini-recorder to capture every word the very big man said. Gaby nodded seriously throughout the brief update. But Lizzie . . . well, Lizzie was thinking of another time. A month or so earlier—in another world, before the dizzy spells and the MRIs and the seizures—she had been standing in the kitchen making toast. She had dropped a small jar of orange marmalade. The jar had shattered into pieces on the floor.

"Stand still," Mike had shouted. "You don't have shoes on. I do. I'll get it."

It was a vigorous cleanup—broom

and dustpan and dish towels and Fantastik spray to finish up.

"Can I move yet?" Lizzie had asked.

Now standing in the hospital, Lizzie remembered Mike's answer.

"Absolutely," he said. "It's perfect. *I think I got it all.*"

Chapter 20

Mike came home and, other than taking long morning and afternoon naps, he was doing well. He walked around the neighborhood, a little wobbly, but he walked. He talked to neighbors, occasionally forgetting a name or two, but he talked. Lizzie crossed her fingers, and hoped for the best.

Then at five o'clock one morning, everything in their world crashed.

At first Lizzie wasn't sure what was happening, but she knew it wasn't a dream, not even a nightmare.

The short, sharp grunting noises, the

gasping for air, the shaking mattress. Mike was having a seizure. He lay on his back, saliva encircling his mouth. His bare legs shot up, then out. For a moment he was calm. Then his right arm twisted horribly and flailed, and his wrist banged hard against the nightstand. Whenever his eyes opened, they rolled aimlessly around in the sockets.

Lizzie did what the head nurse at Mass. General had taught her to do.

She pushed Mike onto his side to help his breathing. She checked his mouth to make sure he had nothing in there. She moved the nightstand and the bedside lamp out of his way.

She watched every tortured breath, every stunted movement. She was terrified; worse, she knew poor Mike had to be terrified too.

Then she heard footsteps in the hall and Tallulah yelling "Mommy? What's that noise?" By the time Tallulah ran into the bedroom, Mike's seizure had ended. He lay there calmly, covered in perspiration, looking as if he'd been dropped onto his bed from an airplane.

"Daddy!" Tallulah cried out when she saw her father.

"Daddy's sick, honey," Lizzie said. "Nothing too bad."

Mike's voice sounded full of gravel as he said, "I guess I ruined your sleepy time, Tallu, huh?" He tried to smile. "But you love the lake, don't you, Tallu? Well, I love the Adirondacks too. You've got to dry off, though. It gets so cold up here."

"Mommy," Tallulah shouted, "Daddy's talking make-believe!"

Then Mike relaxed. He stopped talking. And at that moment Lizzie decided they were going to the hospital. In a hurry.

"Tallulah, call Gaby and tell her to meet us in the emergency room at Stockbridge Hospital. Make sure you say Stockbridge. I don't want her going to the wrong hospital. Tell her I'll call her from the car," Lizzie said.

"Mike, we've got to get over to the hospital. Do you understand?"

"Yes," he said softly. "Of course I do."

"We've got to get you into the bathroom. I'll clean you up. Do you understand that?"

"Lizzie," he said. "I've got cancer in my brain, not in my ear."

She smiled at him. Would there ever be a time when he wouldn't be a joker? *God, she hoped not.*

Chapter 21

"Maybe we should trade in the Hyundai and get an ambulance," Mike said and forced a grin.

Lizzie glanced over at him. Always with the jokes. Mike was wrapped in a thick thermal blanket, his head propped up on a pillow she had grabbed from their bed. The pillow—pale blue with a border of yellow roses—looked silly, as did Mike with a thick blue woolen cap pulled over his head.

"Don't talk. Be still."

"Okay," he said. "I read somewhere

that cancer often disappears if you just sit very still."

Lizzie smiled, and again, just for a moment, she took her eyes away from the dark, icy road and looked at him. Mike didn't look frail at the moment. The blanket gave him a bulky appearance, and his face was puffy from the cortisone they'd been pumping into him.

Then she turned to the backseat and gave Tallulah a smile. "Hang in there, honey," she said.

Her phone rang, and she handed it to Mike.

"Can you answer this?" she asked. "It'll probably be Gaby."

He wiggled his hand out from under the blanket and answered, "Rodgers Cancer Taxi Service. Brain tumors our specialty."

A pause, then, "Gaby, how are you doing?" Another pause. "Oh, we're just out for an early-morning ride in our Hyundai. Catching the fresh air. Yeah. Okay. Yeah. Okay. Looking forward to it. See you there. 'Bye."

He handed the phone back to Lizzie.

"Your mom and Tom Hayden are already at the hospital. They'll meet us outside ER."

"Tom's with Gaby," Lizzie said, and was about to comment on how interesting it was that the two of them were together, but she didn't get the chance. A scream came from the passenger seat. The garbling, gurgling, horrid sounds of another seizure began to explode.

Maybe it was Lizzie's imagination, but this time it seemed louder and wilder and longer. Maybe Mike's being confined by the seatbelt and shoulder belt made his flailing seem more intense than back at home.

From a distance she could see the long, low red brick building that was Stockbridge Hospital. She thought she might have to pull to the side of the road, but she decided that the emergency room was the safest place for Mike right now.

In the nearly empty parking lot she saw Gaby and Tom Hayden. Lizzie screeched to a halt, skidding in a complete circle, like the second hand of a clock, then stopping.

As Tom yanked open the passenger

door, Lizzie shouted, "He's having another seizure."

The moment she said the words, the seizure seemed to stop. Mike's eyes closed, then opened. His face was smeared with sweat again. He rubbed his wrist, sore from where he'd banged it so many times on the armrest.

Tom and Gaby managed to lift Mike out of the car. He stood by himself.

"I'll get a wheelchair," said Lizzie. Tallulah clung to her hand.

"No," said Gaby. "Mike can make it. Right, Mike?" It was as if she were returning a tiny bit of dignity to him. And it worked.

Walking slowly, Mike turned to his wife.

"Lizzie, just look at me. I'm a mess. You've got to do something about your driving."

Chapter 22

Sometimes Gaby felt that she knew the emergency waiting room of Stockbridge Hospital better than she knew her own house.

Not only had she been here a half dozen times during the last year with Mike and Lizzie, but, as the mother of four, she had waited in this same room while Claire had broken fingers set and taped (a diving-board accident), while Seth had twenty-nine stitches in his right thigh (a fall from the hayloft with a perfect landing on a pitchfork), while Lizzie got three hypodermic shots of antihistamine (she was four years old and had punched a beehive), while Emily had a stubbornly stuck tampon removed.

Finally, it was also right here that she had waited as a CPR unit tried to bring Peter back to life when he had his heart attack.

She thought about that horrible day as she walked into the cramped cubicle where they were keeping Mike for the time being.

The sweet, brave guy was wearing one of those ridiculous hospital gowns. Pathetic, Gaby thought. Hospitals got it so wrong. They made being sick even more depressing and depersonalizing than it had to be.

"Sorry to have messed up the morning for you and Tom," Mike said. There was a definite teasing tone in his voice. But Gaby wasn't biting.

"Don't be annoying. The whole gang was there getting breakfast ready. Tom and I were the least important. How are you feeling?" she asked.

"I could swim the Housatonic River north to south," Mike said.

Gaby shook her head. She could only imagine how frightened Mike must be—of cancer and pain and the whole ugly business of being sick and possibly dying. So Gaby did what she was famous for. She asked the simplest, most straightforward question she could think of.

"Mike, are you scared?"

"Would you pass me my clothes?" he said.

"Answer me, Mike. Are you frightened? It's a good question."

"Gaby, please hand me my clothes from that chair. I just want to get dressed and go home."

"I'm going to keep asking."

"Where are Lizzie and Tom? Is Tom the one, *Grandma?*"

"First answer my question. Then I'll answer yours. Your *first* question."

Mike pulled the ridiculous hospital gown around him.

"Everybody looks stupid in these nightgowns," he said. "Even a good-looking hunk like me."

Gaby didn't laugh. She didn't even smile.

Then Mike finally said, "No. I'm not frightened. I'm not frightened at all. I know that's crazy. I should be shaking with fear. But I'm not. This sickness has brought me closer to Lizzie than I've been in years. It's shown me that Tallulah is the most wonderful girl in the world. They don't need me at my own store, but I still get some income from the place. I've grown to like the physiotherapy they put me through after the chemo. So, like I said, it's crazy, but I'm not frightened."

Gaby grabbed Mike's clothing from the chair. Another woman would have carried the pile of clothes to him. But not Gaby. She took the pants and the socks and the shirt and the sweater, rolled them into a ball, and threw it at Mike.

"Thanks for answering my question, Mike. It was a wonderful answer. You're a wonderful guy."

"It was the truth," he said. "Now, by the way, you said you'd answer my question if I answered yours."

"Sure, but I can't even remember your question."

"It was *'Who are you going to marry?'*" he said with a completely straight face.

In a high, squeaky, funny voice Gaby said, "I . . . don't . . . think . . . so."

"Damn," Mike said.

"Do you want me to help you get dressed?" Gaby asked.

"You just want to see me naked," Mike said.

"Yeah, that's always been a dream of mine."

"Anyway, I've got underwear on." He lifted the front of his gown to prove it.

"Well, if you're not even naked, then I definitely don't want to help," Gaby said. "Where's the fun in that?"

As they laughed, Tom and Lizzie walked in.

"What are you two up to?" Tom asked.

But they didn't stop laughing.

Lizzie walked over to her husband and kissed him on his completely bald head.

"You look much better, Mike," Lizzie said.

He kissed her on the cheek. "Thanks, sweetheart."

And for just a second her eyes met Mike's eyes, and for just a second they both smiled. And for just a second there was a feeling of hope.

Chapter 23

CLAIRE AND HANK

Where the hell is Hank? Claire's heart was pounding, and she was feeling like a complete fool. She didn't know where he was, only where he was *supposed* to be. In the headmaster's office with her.

"Will Hank be joining us, Claire?"

"He'll be here any minute. He knows he has to be here. Sorry, Paul."

Hank hadn't called. He had probably forgotten that they were meeting with Paul Lussen, headmaster at Oceanside Prep, to discuss the school's "extraordinary" problems with their son Gus.

Where the hell is he? Claire's heart

was beating even harder, and her head was starting to ache.

Claire had reminded Hank this morning. Twice. He'd snapped at her the second time: "I'm not an imbecile, Claire. Contrary to some people's opinion."

"I have another appointment in half an hour. You know how crazy my schedule is just before winter break," Paul said.

She knew. After all, she was the after-school tutor to four students at Oceanside. She knew all the teachers here and they knew her. And Gus.

"Ordinarily I'd say we should reschedule, but there are extraordinary issues surrounding Gus's future that just can't wait any longer," said Paul.

There was that word again. *Extraordinary.*

Where the hell is Hank? This is unacceptable.

"Well," she said, "I guess we can start. I can bring Hank up to speed later."

Paul was a huge supporter of Claire's and her tutoring. But things went even deeper than that. He was also a good friend, so good a friend that he was, in fact, Gus's godfather.

Today Paul was all business. And it made Claire sad that she was sitting opposite a rather stern headmaster instead of the charming, funny friend who had rocked Gus to sleep when he was little.

Paul opened a folder on his desk. Gus's folder.

"It's hard to know where to begin," he said. Then he looked down at the papers. "I take that back. Actually, Gus's record is so . . . unfortunate . . . that I could begin just about anywhere on these pages. So that's what I'll do."

He read out loud: "September fourteenth. Gus Donoghue and Alex Frahm are seen urinating in the drinking fountain at the school practice field . . . September nineteenth. Gus Donoghue is sent to this office, reprimanded for drinking a Heineken—a Heineken beer! Not a Coke! Not bottled water! A Heineken!—during study hall . . ."

Heineken was his father's favorite, Claire thought and cringed.

Paul kept on reading: "October fourth.

Gus Donoghue and Alex Frahm are found smoking pot in the bathroom."

Claire remembered that whenever she used the word "pot" Gus corrected her. "They haven't called it 'pot' in twenty years, Mom. You call it 'weed.'" Claire decided not to update Paul.

"And the grades, Claire. You're aware of Gus's deplorable grades—Math, D. English, C-. French, F. Biology, D. Music, F. Music! Claire, you know what that course is like in this school. All you have to do is show up and listen to some music and you get a B!"

She nodded.

Where the hell is Hank?

"I know, I know. This is why we took Gus out of public school. This is why I came to work here for no salary. So that we could get free tuition for Gus. We couldn't afford a terrific school like this . . ."

Paul interrupted.

"The problem is that one or two of these transgressions might be considered pranks. But with Gus it's a dozen or more things. Gus does something extraordinary every day. Getting stoned. Getting drunk. Cursing at a teacher."

"I'm trying everything, Paul," Claire said. "I help him at night with his assignments. I forbid him to go out with certain friends, like Alex Frahm. I . . ."

Paul stood up behind his desk.

"I think you've just identified the problem, Claire. You keep using the pronoun 'I.'"

Claire knew where he was going with this, but she just listened. What else could she do?

"Claire, where is Hank in all this? Where is he right now? This is an important meeting for Gus. For your entire family. Hank is still part of the family, right?"

Claire knew Paul well enough that she could cry in front of him, but she didn't want to. She absolutely refused to show weakness.

"Listen. The only reason that Gus hasn't been expelled already is because you work here and, well, because I'm your friend, and I know how much you want Gus to succeed. *But this can't go on.* Two teachers won't allow him in their class next semester, and I don't blame them. What's worse—they *adore* Gus. Then you look at the grades. He can't move on to sophomore year with grades like that. You know, Claire, if you can—"

Claire interrupted. "I know, Paul. 'If you can teach the after-school kids and do a good job, why can't you help your own son?'"

Paul nodded. "If there's no improvement after Christmas, then there's no way I can allow Gus to stay here. This breaks my heart too."

Chapter 24

Claire took deep breath after deep breath as she sat in the empty chapel of Oceanside Prep and listened to a Bach cantata on her iPod. It was an old trick of Gaby's. Bach usually soothed her nerves, but this time Johann Sebastian was letting her down. She made an *L* with a thumb and forefinger and touched it to her forehead: *Loser.* That was her.

As soon as the Bach ended, something unfamiliar came through her earphones. Then she remembered. Gus had commandeered her iPod a few

nights before. He said he was determined to blast her into the twenty-first
century.

She laughed. She was suddenly listening to Daft Punk singing "Something
About Us."

**But there's something about us I
want to say
Cause there's something
between us anyway.**

The music, the words, the beat, the
wacky combination of Claire Donoghue
and Daft Punk in a prep school chapel,
made her shake her head. Unfortunately
Daft Punk was no more successful at
soothing her than Bach, but it did make
her think happily of her son. She loved
Gus so much, in spite of himself. Hell,
everybody loved Gus, even the teachers
who were flunking him.

She remembered as a child seeing a
photo of mothers in a visitors' room at a
state penitentiary. She'd asked Gaby
why all those moms went to see their
sons if the sons were criminals. Gaby

had the answer: "Claire, sweetie, love trumps everything."

Claire snapped open the old pocket watch that hung from a gold chain around her neck. Inside was an antique watch face on the right, and on the left a tiny photo of Gaby, age sixteen. Very pretty. With attitude.

"Now you have me with you all the time," Gaby had said when she gave her the watch. "Even when you don't want me there."

Time for class. Her students—Curtis, Andy, Reggie, Timbo (real name Timothy)—would be waiting for her. If she wasn't on time they'd shout "Class canceled!" and take off.

She clicked the watch closed. She upped the volume on the iPod, and Claire and Daft Punk dance-shuffled down to her tutoring classroom.

I'm not a loser. I've just been acting like one.

Chapter 25

Claire's remedial English class was officially called the Supplementary Academic Advancement Program. Today one of her students, Curtis, decided to set her straight about that.

"You know what they call this class? The Academic Dumb-Ass Program."

"That's harsh. Who calls it that?" Claire asked.

"Everybody does," said Timbo. "Even we do sometimes."

"And how much do you care about that?" Claire asked.

"I don't give a shit," said Andy.

"Same here, Mrs. D.," said Reggie.

"So, that's that. Case closed." She knew that another teacher might get angry at the phrase "give a shit," but not her, and especially not today.

"Listen. We have work to do, and we have an hour to do it," she said. "Mr. McCormack is giving a quiz tomorrow. *The Old Man and the Sea.*"

"Thanks for the Christmas present, Mr. Mack," complained Curtis.

"That's how it is," said Claire. "Anyway, let's start with the obvious. Has everyone read the book?"

"I tried, man, but it was fish, fish, fish, water, water everywhere. The marlin was boring. The old guy was worse than boring. The kid was an asshole. I bailed," said Reggie.

"What page did you give up on?"

A pause. All eyes turned toward Reggie.

"Ten?" he said. The others cracked up. Even Claire did. At least these kids were honest.

"Well, I think tonight, instead of watching *Jersey Shore,* you have some reading to do. Everyone take out a piece of paper."

A small moan, but the paper came out. She couldn't help smiling. The boys were tough and could be disrespectful, but she liked being with them most days.

"First question. What country does Santiago come from?" Claire asked.

"Ms. Donoghue . . ."

"No more talking, Timothy. We've got work to do," Claire said.

Timbo ignored her order and spoke again.

"There's a man at that little window on the door. He looks like he wants to talk to you *real bad.* Is that your husband?"

Chapter 26

"I know that I'm early for our four-thirty," Hank said when Claire met him outside the classroom. "Where should I wait? Outside Paul's office?"

She spat out her next words:

"Our meeting with Paul was at *two-thirty!*"

"You told me four-thirty, Claire. You said so this morning."

"It's been on the calendar all week. I know I said a dozen times that it was *before* my tutoring class. I always said it was *two-thirty.* And I *know* that's what I said this morning."

Claire knew how conniving Hank could be. She knew this was a trick. And she called him on it.

"You knew it was two-thirty. But you forgot. So you thought if you showed up here and pretended that . . . Oh, Jesus . . . I can't believe you."

"That's not what happened," he said. "I swear to God, Claire."

"I don't believe you," she finally said. "You're lying to my face."

"Then fuck you. How's that?" Hank said. At that precise moment Mrs. Rupp, a history teacher, passed by. Mrs. Rupp nodded and walked a little faster.

"Well, that was just terrific. You've made another fan. And look at you. Filthy jeans and a sweaty, smelly shirt. I'd be surprised if you weren't stoned. Are you stoned?"

"You know I've been helping out selling Christmas trees and wreaths down at the nursery. It's a job, Claire."

"And you couldn't change your shirt for a school meeting? No, I still say I don't believe you."

"Yeah? And I still say fuck you."

Claire returned to the classroom and

closed the door behind her. Within seconds Hank was banging on the door. The students looked vaguely frightened so Claire opened it quickly.

"Are you crazy?" she whispered. "With you acting like a madman they may not wait until after Christmas to throw Gus out."

"They're going to throw him out?"

"That's what Paul told me. Too bad you weren't there to hear it."

"Did Paul say what we should do?"

She backed away from Hank. She stood in the doorway, shaking her head.

"Yeah. Actually he did. Paul said we should try to find Gus a father."

GABY'S FOURTH VIDEO— JACOB'S MOTTO

Hey. Everyone okay out there? I have a story to tell you—about one of your favorite people. Jacob.

Last week he and I were having dinner together, and he reminded me that I'd never heard him give a sermon. I said that he'd never invited me to his temple.

And the next thing you know it was Saturday morning, and there I was in the fifth row.

I saw a Jacob I'd never seen before. What an incredible person he is—even better than I had thought.

The cantor stopped singing. The congregation sat down. Jacob walked to the front of the altar and faced us.

He wore a long black robe, almost like an old-fashioned college professor's gown, a yarmulke, and a tallis. Maybe I'm being sacrilegious, but I've got to say Jacob looked great—with his jet-black hair, his scruffy two-day beard and—okay, let me get to the sermon.

Jacob grabbed everybody with his opening line and powerfully understated delivery:

"In case you didn't know this already, let me be the first to tell you:

"Nobody in this temple is going to live forever, nobody on this earth is going to live forever."

A few in the congregation laughed. But more of us looked a little surprised.

He went on to talk about how each of us has a life that has to be lived. How it makes no difference if you're CEO of a huge company or the guy who slices cold cuts at the deli. Jacob said he was amazed at how parents became obsessed about colleges, but it doesn't make much difference to God if your daughter goes to Harvard or the Springfield School of Beauty.

For me the surprise was that Jacob was so passionate. His voice got deeper and the rhythms got faster. I could feel my hands sweating. It was a good thing.

He came to the end and started talking about seizing the life we were given. Jacob didn't say "Seize the day," he said "Seize what's been handed you." Make smart decisions. Make decisions because—he said it again—life is a temporary situation.

He ended with a prayer usually said on Yom Kippur. I had never heard it before. It was beautiful, and he gave me a copy afterward.

Jacob looked exhausted after the service. His face was shiny with sweat. He said he needed to unwind and asked if I would join him.

He took me out to his garage. The door opened, and there was the coolest old Mustang. Navy blue, a '65 convertible, and the top was already down.

Next thing, Jacob and I were speeding along Under Mountain Road. He was going seventy, seventy-five miles an hour. And he was very intense, very focused. He looked like a French movie star, like Jean-Paul Belmondo or Romain Duris. He drove faster. I looked at the speedometer, and it was reading ninety. I realized Jacob was driving the same way he gave his sermon. He started small and casual, then he built up speed, and eventually he was flying . . . ninety . . . ninety-five . . . a hundred.

Between the passionate sermon, and the beautiful car, and the high-speed drive on a country road, I saw that a man I liked immensely had turned into a man I . . . I . . . well, I think I've told everyone enough to get their imaginations churning.

Before I stop this tape, let me just read a few lines from the prayer Jacob gave me.

**On Yom Kippur it is sealed.
How many shall pass away and
  how many shall be born,
Who shall live and who shall die,
Who shall reach the end of his
  days and who shall not.**

Listen, I've got to go. All of you remember what Jacob said: We're not going to live forever. So, kids, please do
yourselves a favor: *Seize life!*

I'm going to. And so, I suspect, is Jacob.

GABY'S FIFTH VIDEO— MARTY'S VISIT

So we're getting ready to serve breakfast to the homeless—Lord, are we nice
people or what?—and your uncle Marty
looks up from the peaches he's chopping for the granola, and he says, "What
is bothering you so badly, Gaby?"

And I say, "How'd you know something was up?"

He says, "I know you, Gaby. Maybe

better than anyone. I can see pain in your eyes. It's obvious to me."

So I told him that my junior class was bugging the shit out of me. I told Marty they were all so good at figuring out how to get great grades on their book reports that they essentially ignored the books. You know, how you can read *To Kill a Mockingbird* or *The Things They Carried* and completely understand the book but not in any way *feel* the book?

And to my amazement, Marty says, "How about I come by and talk to the kids?" I was thrilled.

So, at ten o'clock that same morning, when they all file in—pulling their earphones out of their ears, hiding their Cokes—they see me standing in the back of the room and Marty sitting on my desk facing the class.

I tell them to settle down. I tell them Marty is a good friend and that he's going to teach the class. And, of course, Tara Walsh raises her hand and asks, "Is there going to be a quiz on your friend's talk?"

Marty says, "Yeah. So you'd better

pay attention. The quiz counts for ninety percent of your final grade."

"Ninety-eight percent," I quip from the back.

Then he dives right in. No small talk. No "Good morning, everyone." Just this man standing there in faded jeans and a denim shirt that cost more than an iPod, talking in a tough, confident voice.

He points at a boy slouched over in back and says, "What's your favorite book, dude?"

No answer at first. Marty just stares, and finally the boy says, "I guess it's sort of for littler kids, but, to be honest, the only book I ever really liked was *Diary of a Wimpy Kid.*"

Marty says, "Of course you liked it. It's a terrific book, funny as hell. I guess my favorite part is when Fregley slips a letter under Greg's door. I actually remember the letter: 'Dear Gregory, I'm very sorry I chased you with a booger on my finger. Here, I put it on this paper so you can get me back.'"

A lot of the class laughs. Then Marty points to another kid, who looks like he's texting.

"What's your favorite book?" The kid doesn't even know he's being spoken to. He just keeps on texting.

Another kid, Mia Wendel, calls out, "The last book Joey read was *Goodnight Moon.*"

Marty says, "Another very good book, one of my favorites."

Then Marty says something like "Listen. Twenty-five years from now, believe it or not, you all will be forty years old. And you know when twenty-five years is? It's tomorrow. That's how fast it happens. And I'll tell you something: If you're not reading—with your heart as well as your brain—you will be one stupid grown-up. Even worse, you'll be missing out on one of the best experiences you can possibly have. Nowhere will you meet more interesting people than in books. I've met a lot of people, I've read a lot of books, and that's the absolute truth."

And I realize that I'm sitting there enthralled, listening as intently as the kids are.

"It doesn't make a bit of difference how you read—a Kindle, an iPad, a book-book. Read a graphic novel if you like them. Read a biography of somebody awful—Hitler or Lee Harvey Oswald. I can see that not all of you know who Lee Harvey Oswald is. He shot John Kennedy."

Then Marty says, "Okay. Next question: What's the absolutely worst book you ever read?"

Suddenly there's a heated debate. Which was worse, *Moby-Dick* or *Pride and Prejudice*? This one's closer than Gore versus Bush. So Marty says, "Let's settle it this way. Do most of you agree they both sucked?"

All but the brownnosers agree. And Marty says, "When you're home tonight, look at them again. Open them up anywhere. Start to read. You already know the stories.

"And let's say you get to an exceptionally boring part of *Moby-Dick,* like the part where Melville writes twenty pages on how they drain the whale oil. Read it slowly. Even if it's painful. Then close the book and think about what you just read. Think about how the whalers did it. How they worked, how the blood sprayed them until their eyes hurt. How they slid and slithered off the whale.

"You see, one of the best things about reading is that you'll always have something to think about when you're *not* reading.

"Okay, try the same thing with the Jane Austen. But do me a favor: think of *Pride and Prejudice* as something meant to be funny. *Pride and Prejudice* is friggin' funny."

Someone yells out, "Yeah, man. *Pride and Prejudice* is just like *Family Guy.* Hope I don't get the two of 'em confused."

Marty says, "Hey, listen. Maybe you're right. Maybe you'll still think it's boring. You don't have to like everything. I'm that way. I'd rather have root canal than read *A Tale of Two Cities,* but give me another one of Dickens's books, like *Oliver Twist,* and I'll stay up all night."

Now I'm thinking that I should have Marty go to every class in the school—from chemistry to shop to computer science—and give this talk. And I'm also thinking that I learned things about books and reading that I'd never thought of, and I'm also thinking that . . . that . . . my brother-in-law is just about the smartest person I know.

When the bell rings there's a really big, really honest round of applause. Kids come up and pump Marty's hand and pat him on the back. Tara Walsh asks again if there's going to be a quiz. I *think* Tara is kidding.

I was on break after that class. So I brought Marty to the cafeteria and got him some awful coffee. Then we went outside and took a walk around the basketball court. I thanked him for coming. He told me it was nothing, a total pleasure. We circled the basketball court two more times. Marty put his arm around my shoulder.

I said to him that we probably looked like two middle-aged lovers.

He looked at me and said, "Maybe we are and we just don't know it yet."

Talk to you later, guys. See you on Christmas—*soon.*

When all will be revealed.

Chapter 27

GABY, STACEY LEE, TOM, MARTY, AND JACOB

Jacob held a small, crisp piece of whole-grain ciabatta bread an inch from his mouth. On the ciabatta was a slice of foie gras. On top of the foie gras was a paper-thin layer of chocolate, and on top of the chocolate was the tiniest glob of jellied wine—a Sauternes.

"You look like a little kid about to take his cod-liver oil," said Tom, who was wearing one of his old Flyers sweatshirts and still looked like a first-string athlete.

Jacob put the food in his mouth and cringed. Suddenly his fearful expression

changed to one of almost dreamy ec-
stasy. He closed his eyes and chewed
slowly. Finally he spoke.

"Now I know what the angels eat for
dinner."

"Wrong religion, Jacob," said Marty.
"But probably true."

This was the food tasting and food
testing for the wedding reception. Tough
duty. They would be selecting from
among several wines: red, white, sparkling. Stacey Lee had prepared twelve
hors d'oeuvres, from which they were to
choose four. She and Gaby had prepared eight entrees. Three of them were
poultry—guinea hen with olives and ca-
pers; chicken breast with goat cheese;
coq au vin with Riesling ("An old Lutèce
thing that no one ever gets tired of,"
Stacey Lee said). Another three were
seafood—chunks of lobster between
layers of puff pastry; wild sea bass with
braised fennel; Cajun shrimp and craw-
fish with "careless dabs of red and black
caviar." Finally, there were two vegetar-
ian dishes—a plate of miniature patty-
pan squash, miniature yellow squash,
miniature lima beans, and miniature

scallions ("I thought scallions were miniature onions to begin with," said Marty) and homemade spinach fettuccine with a porcini sauce.

"These are the best twenty meals I ever ate at one sitting," said Tom. "Just like the old training table in Philly."

The men couldn't get enough food. At one point Marty and Tom actually raised their voices over who got the last mouthful of sea bass. (They split it.)

"If the wedding's half as good as the food tasting, then you've got a hit on your hands," Marty said. "You and *whoever.* Whatever, whichever."

The only problem was that they couldn't come to an agreement about what should be eliminated from the final menu.

At that point—just when they were about to compare all-chocolate desserts with a grouping of fruit tarts with rosemary sorbet—Tom said, "I offer my services, free of charge, to be your store's official taster."

"I don't think my accountant would allow it," Stacey Lee said. The friends were definitely feeling rosy and happy.

Only Gaby was quiet. Whenever Stacey Lee asked her what dishes she preferred, she smiled and said, "Oh, you guys decide. I'm too nervous. It's all good."

As they all walked to their cars, Gaby took Marty aside. "Stay a minute? I have to ask you something."

Chapter 28

Marty and Gaby walked back along the icy driveway to the house. Marty tried to take her arm, but she pulled away.

I'm tired of touching people and being touched by people, Gaby was thinking. All the kissing and hugging and squeezing and hand-holding. *Maybe I was born to end up alone. Maybe I should cancel the wedding right now.*

She and Marty walked into the kitchen. He was smart enough not to intrude on her thoughts, to just be there. Stacey Lee was scraping dishes, rinsing wineglasses, and then putting them into heavy plastic cartons.

"We'll help," Gaby volunteered.

"No need. I just have to get these rinsed off. One of the indentured servants from the store will pick them up tomorrow to wash."

Gaby smiled. "Total efficiency. I love it." So she and Marty headed off to the living room.

"Okay, what's wrong?" he asked.

"Nothing," Gaby said. Then she went on, "Oh, everything. Marty, I have to ask you something, and you have to be honest."

"Shoot. I'm always honest with you."

"Okay. Well. You knew Peter better than anyone else. You were practically twins. So, I need to ask you this question. *Am I doing the right thing?*"

Marty thought about it before he said anything. "I can't answer that. Only *you* can answer that."

"Okay. Fair enough."

Marty realized that his response had disappointed her. That wasn't what he'd wanted to do.

"No, Gaby, I won't give you an answer. But I will give you an opinion. And here it is: *No! No! No!* Peter would definitely not mind. He'd be happy. Peter would be happy, because getting married is going to make *you* happy. And he loved to make you happy more than anything else in his life."

Gaby's eyes instantly filled with tears. "Thank you, Marty."

"Remember, it wasn't an answer. It was an opinion."

Suddenly she felt the need to hug him. "Do you mind terribly . . . the way I'm doing this? Making it ladies' choice?"

Marty looked into her eyes. "No. I don't mind at all. Do you know why? Because I love to make you happy too."

Chapter 29

EMILY AND BART

The year before, Dale, Hardy had held its Christmas party at New York's chic restaurant Eleven Madison Park. The law firm booked the entire restaurant. They had two martini bars, poured twelve cases of Opus One, and served nigiri sushi, organic beef carpaccio, and blini with caviar.

The party cost $400,000.

This year, money was tighter. So less luxury was the solution. No restaurant. The Christmas party would be held at the Dale, Hardy offices. They would still have two martini bars, pour twelve cases of Opus One, and serve nigiri sushi, organic beef carpaccio, and blini with caviar.

It would cost a mere $250,000.

"I like having it here at the factory better," said Jason McIntyre, an up-and-coming young attorney who had graduated from Columbia Law with Emily. "More money for bonuses. Nobody believes in Christmas anyway."

"I think it's more festive when you go out someplace," said Emily. "And actually I believe in Christmas."

"Yeah, I'll bet you do, Em," said Jason. "But as long as you're at the office, you can sneak away and get some work done."

Emily knew that her distaste for Jason's usual cynicism showed on her face. She excused herself and got a white wine spritzer, which she probably wouldn't drink. What a scene. What a hackneyed stupid scene. Emily felt like she had walked into the wrong movie.

Jeanne Gallery, a promising Stanford Law graduate and junior associate, was exchanging lingering kisses with Ben Abbots, a promising Yale Law graduate who had just married his girlfriend over Thanksgiving weekend. That completely turned Emily's stomach.

The handsome, and married, head of wills and estates, Danny Josephson, had his hand planted firmly on the back-side of the handsome, also married Spanish-document translator, Raymond Ramirez.

Old Man Hardy sat on a large ma-hogany chair, actually a throne, beneath his own portrait, as a multitude of office toadies flocked around him as if he were an aging rock star. Keith Richards looked better than Hardy these days, and the Rolling Stones guitarist was ac-tually older by two years.

"Have yourselves a merry little Christ-mas," Emily muttered as she moved on.

Then she heard the familiar baritone of her boss, Cliff Church. "Pretty motley crew, huh, Em?"

"Christmas Manhattan style. Kind of brings out the small-town girl in me," Emily said. Her voice was barely audible over the blaring gangsta rap, urban mu-sic that failed totally at transforming this into a cool party.

"Come on over to my office," Cliff said. "I've got something that'll brighten your holidays. I promise."

Only one word came to Emily's mind: "Partner." Maybe this wasn't such a lousy Christmas party after all.

Chapter 30

"I should have done this earlier in the day, but you were in meeting after meeting," said Cliff. "A typical Emily Summerhill afternoon."

He reached into the drawer in the console behind his desk, the one where he displayed the photos of his lovely wife and his equally dazzling blond sons. He removed a white business envelope and handed it to Emily. "Merry Christmas, Em."

"Thank you," she said. "Merry Christmas to you."

"Go ahead, open it," Cliff said. He was smiling a nervous smile.

And so she did, and removed a check made out to her in the amount of $150,000. It was a big chunk of change. But it wasn't the magic word. She was confused, but, to her amazement, she wasn't angry. She was hurt. She was sad. She was silent.

"I don't mind telling you, Em, that's a generous bonus. There aren't many that size being handed out this year at your level."

She wanted to say, "But I thought I was being made partner?" Instead she remained silent. She had never been a whiner.

Cliff couldn't bear the silence. He decided to fill it with his own pompous voice.

"This has not been the best year in the history of Dale, Hardy," he said. "The economy remains dicey. They're letting people go. Everyone who works here is scared. Even the Cliffster."

Still, Emily said nothing.

Cliff kept going: "My unfailing insight

tells me that you're disappointed that you weren't made partner. I know you feel you had it coming, and I agree. Absolutely. You work your perfect ass off. Maybe . . . maybe a little too much pro bono work . . ." He paused for a phony-sounding chuckle. "But you're definitely a rising star. You're a terrific lawyer. Like I said, you work hard."

She knew Cliff wanted her to start talking, but honestly, she was just too damned sad to start chattering away. Something about the night, the party, the *Christmas* party. Maybe even the fact that Gaby was getting married to God knew who.

"You know, the firm just isn't making commitments. I'm sure that when Old Man Hardy appoints the next group of partners, your name will be at the very top."

Then she spoke. Softly. Politely. "It *is* a disappointment. But the bonus is very generous."

"Yes, it is. I'm glad you realize that," Cliff said as he shut the console drawer and walked around to Emily's side of the desk. He put his arm around her shoulder and added, "My own bonus wasn't a lot more."

Oh, she thought. So we both got shitty bonuses, and I didn't get partner. And now your hand is slipping down my back, lingering at my bra strap, and about to land on my butt.

"That's reassuring," she said. Emily wasn't sure Cliff recognized the sarcasm in her voice.

His hand was now firmly established on what he had just called her "perfect ass," and he stepped in and held himself firmly against her. So, this was Christmas. This was Dale, Hardy. This was her life.

If this were a movie, she would have slapped him. But instead, with her heart full of confusion, she stepped to the side and was free of her boss.

"Cliff, I'm glad we had a chance to get some time alone," she said. And Emily saw that his eyes sparkled at the thought of Yuletide sex.

"Me too," he said.

She looked him directly in the eyes.

"There's something I need to tell you."

Chapter 31

On her way home, Emily played the moment over and over in her mind. "I'm leaving Dale, Hardy, effective immediately," she'd said, and Cliff had actually laughed in her face.

"You don't believe me? It's true. I'm leaving, effective immediately," she had said, and Cliff had finally looked confused, totally off his game, for a split second.

"And to prove my point, I'm leaving this office, and this terrifying party."

A half hour later, Emily was walking through the door of her empty apartment. She removed her party dress. She poured herself a Coke. And then she did what every Summerhill child did when there was a crisis: She called Gaby.

She told her about the conversation with Cliff, and God bless her, Gaby said *exactly* what Emily needed to hear.

"That's the best news I've heard all week."

"It is?"

"Absolutely. Listen, Emily. Being a partner at a big-deal law firm is terrific, I guess ... *to someone else* ... not to you, and certainly not to me. Let me just tell you this: I'm proudest when you tell me you got a poor guy out of jail when he was sentenced unfairly," Gaby said. "And that's not me being a sap, that's me being human, that's me being me."

What was there in Gaby's voice that brought such wonderful peace to her children? That was the question all four of them always asked.

"I appreciate everything you've said, Mom. I really, really do. You're the best."

"I just say what I think."

Maybe that was the source of Gaby's

kindness. There was a simple truth and decency to their mother that added strength and wisdom to whatever she said.

"And what does Bart think about all this?" Gaby finally asked.

A long pause.

"He doesn't know."

"Wow. You *are* the spunky one."

"Was I wrong not to have discussed it with him?"

"What difference does it make now? The ship has sailed. Where is Dr. Perfect, anyway?"

"He's working tonight too. On call. He thought I'd be late at the party, and . . ."

"So go and drink a big cup of tea or a big glass of your beloved high-octane Coca-Cola, watch Turner Classics, and get a good night's sleep. Then tomorrow you can get up here nice and early for my wedding."

"Oh, while I'm thinking of it, Bart and I aren't sure when exactly we're going to show up, but we'll definitely be there by Christmas Eve Day."

"Why so late? It's not like you have a job to go to," Gaby said. They both laughed then, and Gaby said, "I do have one more thing to say."

"I'll take a wild guess. It's about what I'll be wearing to your wedding."

"You're a mind reader. Emily, it's my only request: Please wear something festive. Not some deadly gray or dark blue Prada thing. This is not Manhattan, you know."

"I was thinking of a yellow gingham dirndl."

"Perfect. Good night, sweetie."

"Oh, wait. There's one other thing. Who did you say you were marrying?" Emily asked.

"Oh, Emily. You are so bad at cross-examination. It's a good thing you left that law firm. Bye-bye. See you in my dreams."

"Always, Mom. And thank you. I'm sure tonight I'll see you in my dreams too."

Chapter 32

Rest, Emily. Rest.

As she stood in the kitchen carefully measuring out two perfectly rounded teaspoons of decaf Assam tea, Emily heard a voice coming from the living room.

"A ten-second warning to whoever is in the kitchen." It was gruff. It was loud. It was Bart.

She turned to face the kitchen doorway, and there he stood. His face was red from the cold. She could tell that under his ski parka he was still wearing his baby-blue scrubs.

He held a bottle of champagne in one hand and a bouquet of long-stemmed white roses in the other. There was her guy. Just in the nick of time.

He put the champagne and roses on the counter and walked to her quickly. He kissed her long and hard. Apparently one kiss was not nearly enough, so he repeated his actions. Only then did he pull back and speak.

"Well?" he asked as he held her shoulders.

"I received a lovely bonus."

"Great. Congratulations. And . . . ?"

"And?" she asked with mock innocence.

"And are you now a partner at Dull, Farty?" The name was Bart's ongoing joke about the pretentious firm.

Slowly and firmly, emphasizing each word, Emily said, "I . . . am . . . not."

Another husband might have dropped his arms from her shoulders and stepped back. But, as Gaby kidded, Bart was Dr. Perfect. So instead, he pulled her close.

"Em, that sucks big time. I'm sorry. I

am so sorry. You worked so hard. You are so talented."

"Would you believe me if I said—I don't care."

"If the words come from your mouth, then I know it's the truth."

"Want some tea?" she asked.

"I'll have some of yours," he said.

They walked into the living room. She sat on the couch and Bart lay down, resting his head on her lap. He turned his head to one side and enjoyed the soft skin of her thigh against his cheek. He rubbed her lovely bare leg. "Peach fuzz. I love peach fuzz," he said.

"So, as you know, the party was in the office . . . up on thirty-five . . . where there's that huge corridor with all the fancy conference rooms off it. And they had this guy, DJ Nini, blasting music, and I'm sure a lot of people were having a fabulous time. But there was also the undercurrent of politics and the under-current of sex and the . . . Oh, Bart. I just didn't want to be there. And that's because . . . because . . . *I didn't belong there. I wasn't like them. They weren't like me.* I absolutely *looked* like them. But I was different inside . . ."

She breathed in the steam from her tea.

"Be careful with that tea," Bart said. "If you spill it on my face . . . you'll . . . you'll . . ." He was searching for the words.

Emily supplied them: "You'll lose your boyish good looks."

"Yeah. That's it. Anyway. What happened next?"

"Cliff asked me to come into his office, and . . ." She paused. She was searching for the words.

Bart supplied them: "And he made a pass at you, of course."

"How'd you know?"

"Lucky guess. What else could make the evening absolutely perfect?"

"So he handed me a bonus check. He hemmed and hawed and pretended to be sorry that I hadn't made partner, and then . . ." She paused again. And for the final time that evening Bart supplied the words:

"And you quit."

Then he kissed her again. Gaby was right. Dr. Perfect.

"We're going to Stockbridge for Christmas?" she asked.

"Absolutely. Gaby's getting married. Who in their right mind would miss that?"

Chapter 33

ANDIE AND SETH

"I swear to God, this little heap of junk has more miles on it than Apollo Eleven," Andie said as they drove their old Chevy Cav across the Mass. Pike "from Boston to Stockbridge"—just the reverse of the old song "Sweet Baby James."

Andie's nickname for the car was Popcorn because of its tendency to lurch or backfire unexpectedly. Seth's nickname for it was This Goddamn Piece of Shit.

The car lacked a proper inspection sticker, an emission sticker, and a radio (stolen years before when Popcorn was "resting" in a sketchy area of Baltimore). Since the radio and cassette player were gone, Seth had hooked up his iPod to two small speakers and taped the speakers to the genuine plastic dashboard.

He and Andie sang along with Mýa and Pras to "Ghetto Supastar":

I'ma teach this cat
how to live in the ghetto

As they headed past Framingham they saw that a significant amount of snow was coming down. Nothing to do but crack open a warm Guinness, and keep singing.

They allowed Mya to solo a little too. Seth handed the Guinness to Andie. He clearly needed both hands on the wheel. He leaned forward and squinted hard into the heavily falling snow.

"I hate This Goddamn Piece of Shit car," he shouted over the music. "The first thing I was going to do when I sold my book was buy us a luxurious used Honda."

"Stay calm, sweetie," Andie said. "Like your mother says, we're still kids. We've got time to be big shots."

"I don't want to be a big shot," Seth replied. "I just want to sell a book. I want a few people to take it to bed at night. I want a few ladies in North Dakota to discuss it at their book club. I just . . ."

At that exact moment a truck the size of a house jackknifed right in front of Popcorn.

Seth turned the steering wheel away from the monster truck, and then he found himself flipped around and facing oncoming traffic and dozens of head-lights. The skid seemed endless and very fast. He did everything a driver *wasn't* supposed to do. He slammed on the brakes. He turned in the opposite di-rection of the skid.

Andie was frozen with fear. And, of course, all she could think was *We're going to die exactly like my parents did. Exactly.*

Then it happened. Suddenly. Unex-pectedly. Miraculously.

Andie and Seth and This Goddamn

Piece of Shit were sitting safely on the snowy shoulder of the Mass. Pike.

Shaking, they reached for each other. They were safe. They held each other, hugged for a long time.

Popcorn, on the other hand, seemed none the worse for the wear and terror. As if to signal the car's good health, the speakers suddenly began blaring a song by the Black Eyed Peas.

"Wow. A fatal accident sure would have hurt the good vibe at your mom's wedding," Andie said quietly.

"Well, I certainly hope so," said Seth. "*Near* fatal. Not a problem." Then they both laughed, nervously, but there was laughter.

Seth eased the car very cautiously back onto the Mass. Pike.

"Hey, I've got an idea," Andie said.

"What's that?" he said.

"Let's turn off the iPod and sing Christmas carols, like 'Jingle Bells' or 'I Saw Mommy Kissing Santa Claus.'"

"Good idea," Seth said. "I just wish I knew which Santa Claus my mommy is going to be kissing."

And so Seth and Andie sang Christmas songs.

And then they did something even more unexpected but definitely in the spirit of the season.

Now they had a very cool surprise of their own.

Chapter 34

CLAIRE AND HANK

Two nights earlier, Claire had done the hardest, most awful thing she'd ever had to do: She told Hank to get out of the house. She shook as she said it, but she said it. And Hank got out. He saw the tears in Claire's eyes, but he also saw the anger and the resolve, and maybe even the hurt he'd caused.

"She'll get over it, Dad. She always does," Gus said as he helped Hank put a duffel bag and a six-pack of Heineken in the car.

"Yeah," Hank said. "I'll sweet-talk my way back before Christmas. You stand strong, now. You're the man while I'm gone."

"I know that, Dad. I'm the man."

Then Hank made a foolish error: He went back inside the house to try to kiss Claire. She turned away and walked quickly out of the kitchen.

But she did hear him shout, "Just remember, you're the bitch who threw me out of here. You're the bitch who ruined our family's Christmas."

The twins, Toby and Gabrielle, were frightened by Hank's leaving. Gus seemed amused. And Claire hadn't yet told anyone else—not even Gaby—about it.

That night, when she lay alone and upset in bed, she wondered if she *were* the bitch who had ruined Christmas. Couldn't she have waited until the new year? Or given Hank another chance? Should she have found some sort of marriage counselor? And where would Hank go? She almost didn't want to think about that one.

But she didn't have to wait long to find out. The next evening, as she and the children were quietly eating baked macaroni, Hank walked in.

"Look, it's Daddy," Toby yelled, and he and Gabrielle rushed to embrace their father.

"Man, you wasted no time," Gus said, and Hank tousled the boy's hair.

Angry as she was, Claire had to admit that Hank was looking good for a change. Good as in "good and handsome," good as in "good and sexy."

His blond hair was washed and combed into perfect place. He had shaved, and he smelled of a cologne that was his favorite, though not actually hers. White shirt, blue blazer, khaki slacks. The hayseed preppy, she used to call him, and that's exactly what he looked like now.

"May I pull up a chair?" he asked.

He didn't wait for Claire to reply. He simply sat in his usual place and scooped out a portion of baked macaroni—with his hand. But only enough so that it wasn't *too* gross. Just the kind of slapstick that worked every time with the kids.

Hank was all charm, but Claire was

not about to fall for it, not the way she had so many times before. She knew the routine by heart. Hank cleaned himself up, transformed himself into the perfect gentleman, looked as young as one of the surfers over at the Grand Strand Beach.

"Get a *plate,* Daddy," said Gabrielle, laughing at Hank's sloppiness.

Then Claire finally spoke: "You're going to have to leave, Hank."

"Aw, c'mon, Claire. It's Christmas," he said.

Then Hank managed to transport the entire portion of baked macaroni from his hand to his mouth.

"No, Hank. This is it."

He swallowed the huge mouthful before he spoke again. The pause was effective, and excruciating for her.

"Claire. I got the message. I got the news. I've been a total jerk, but it's going to be different from now on. Okay? I got it."

She knew this conversation should not be taking place in front of the children, but she also knew she could not back down now.

"No, it's not okay," she said.

"Mom, give the dude a break," Gus said.

"Yeah, Claire. Give this dude a friggin' break," Hank said.

"Get out, Hank. *Get out now.* You're not welcome here anymore."

Hank stood up and wiped his hand on Toby's napkin. For a moment Claire thought that he might come at her with a fist or a fork or a knife. Instead he walked to the door.

"Good night, guys," he said. "Merry Christmas to one and all."

All three children said "Merry Christmas" in voices soft and nervous. And all Claire could think was *I hope I have the brains to give myself a great Christmas gift. I hope I have the strength not to let him back.* But as she looked at Toby's and Gabrielle's gloomy faces, as she watched the quiver of their lips as they held back tears, Claire wasn't sure she would have the guts to see this through to the end.

But she had to—*she had to have the guts.*

Chapter 35

"Tell your brother I want him down here in ten seconds or less," Claire said to Toby.

It was eight o'clock on a damp Carolina morning, the day after Hank's dinnertime visit. Claire, Toby, and Gabrielle were packing the truck for the long drive to Massachusetts. Claire would be at the wheel, Gus would be riding shotgun, and the twins would be stuck in the jump seats.

"Tell your brother we're ready to leave," Claire repeated.

Toby screamed at the top of his lungs:

"Gussssss! Mom said get down here! We're ready to go!"

"I meant *go upstairs* and tell him to come down," Claire said. "Go on, now. Scoot. I'm waiting on you both."

Then she did what any mother would do—she took out her cell phone and telephoned Gus.

"Gus, I told you that I want to make central Jersey before it gets dark, and we're not going to do it unless we leave right now."

There was a pause. She clicked the phone shut, mumbled the phrase "Son of a bitch," and ran inside, passing Toby along the way.

"We're leaving," she shouted outside Gus's room. "Right now, young man. Toby—get in the truck!"

"Go ahead without me," she heard Gus say.

"Get out here now."

"I'm not going," he shouted back. "I'll go stay with Dad."

"I swear . . . I'll break this door down."

"Go ahead."

Claire took a deep breath, rubbed her

face, and went downstairs and outside. Toby and Gabrielle, rapt, watched her unhook the side compartment of the truck where the spare tire was kept. The twins were wide-eyed as she walked back inside the house.

She was carrying a tire iron.

At Gus's bedroom door, she said, "Last warning."

Gus replied, "Get the fuck away."

And that did it. She held the tire iron high and smashed it against the door.

The wood began to splinter. Claire landed blow after blow after blow with the tire iron. There was now a hole in the door that was larger than her head. Through that hole she saw a very fright-ened-looking Gus.

"Are you ready now?" she said.

"Yes," he said softly.

"We'll be in the truck."

She walked down the stairs. By the time she reached the kitchen she real-ized that her hands were shaking and that her eyes were tearing up. *I'm a mess,* she thought. *I'm an absolute mess. But I do have guts.*

"What's up with Gus?" Gabrielle

asked as Claire climbed into the driver's seat.

"He'll be down in a minute. I finally talked some sense into your brother."

GABY'S SIXTH VIDEO—A WALK WITH TOM

Yesterday, I was headed over to the barn to get breakfast started when my cell phone started ringing.

A phone call at five-thirty in the morning is usually bad news. But not this one. It was Tom, telling me he couldn't make our breakfast group, but asking if I would have lunch with him. I said yes before he even finished the question. And then, of course, I started wondering if there was a problem and what it was that he wanted to talk about.

Tom picked me up around noon. A half hour later we were parked at the entrance to a state park. He pulled out a big cloth shopping bag from the backseat and said, "You up for a picnic in the woods?"

I was. I loved picnics, and I also loved

spending time with Tom. We'd been doing stuff like this since we were kids.

What an unbelievably beautiful day
for late December. Brilliant blue skies,
lots of sun, temp in the low fifties.

Tom has eyes like an eagle. During
our walk he pointed out an otter's den
on the side of a frozen brook and a fat
gray wren starting to build a nest on a
high branch in a bare tree. When the
weather turns suddenly warm, the birds
who stay up north get confused and
think it's spring.

The melting snow made the ground
soggy in most places, but we found a
nice flat boulder that was warmed by
the sun. We spread out a blanket, and
Tom unpacked a bottle of white Bur-
gundy, some salami, and brie and apples and French bread.

The wine loosened my tongue, and I
found myself asking Tom something I'd
always wanted to ask: why he never
talked about the days he played pro
hockey.

He avoided the question again and
said something like "If you skated for

the Flyers in the seventies you don't go bragging about it."

I asked him why. And he said, "Do you know what the Flyers' nickname was back then? The Broad Street Bullies." Tom went on, "We were a bunch of demented animals. We were told that fighting was more important than skating. I started hating the game. So I quit. I broke my share of noses, and my stick was up in the air more than it was down on the ice. But I just couldn't keep doing it."

Tom asked if I felt like walking some more. I would have done just about anything to make the day last longer.

In a few minutes we were in a crab apple orchard. The trees were big and thick and gnarly.

"Come on up with me," he said, and we climbed to the lowest big branch of a tree. He held out his hand for me, and I tried to act like I climbed trees for a living. Then we scrambled up to the next branch and snuggled into a cozy crook.

Now it was late afternoon. The air was getting cold and crisp again. We had a perfect view of the Berkshires in the distance.

Together, Tom and I watched the pale winter sun start to go down. There was no better place to be, and Tom was the right person to be there with.

I think I've said enough for now.

It's almost Christmas.

Yay.

BOOK TWO

The Days Before Christmas

Chapter 36

'Twas the season to be exhausted. And since we were planning Christmas *and* a wedding, well . . . 'twas the season to be *ridiculously* exhausted.

"Listen, guys, I need the string of lights to be more . . . I dunno . . . careless-looking. As if an angel just sort of tossed them up there over the barn doors," I shouted to Tom, who was perched at the top of a very old and shaky wooden ladder.

"Gaby, the reason he's not responding is because his lips have frozen shut," said Jacob, who was holding the

ladder, a bit too casually, I thought. Considering thinning out the competition,
maybe? No, Jacob and Tom were best
friends. They *still* were best friends,
right?

It was seven o'clock in the evening
without a cloud in the black sky. The
New England air was refreshingly clear
and painfully cold. A slightly nervous
bride-to-be, an ex–hockey jock, and a
wisecracking rabbi were finishing the
outdoor decorations.

Stacey Lee and I had already taken
care of the inside of the house—a ma-
jestic ten-foot-tall Christmas tree in the
front hall, evergreen and holly branches
stacked high on the fireplace mantels.
The time-worn stockings I had knitted
for the family years earlier hung by the
chimney without as much care as usual,
because I'd gotten a little sentimental as
I put up Peter's stocking.

Stacey Lee had the sweet common
sense not to say anything. She just
hugged me. Drama was definitely in the
air, wasn't it?

"How's that look?" Tom called down.
He had on another of his hockey sweat-

shirts, or maybe the same one, and he still looked like he could skate up a storm at the drop of a puck.

"Perfect," I shouted back. "Close enough."

"Pull the whole thing a few inches to the right," yelled Jacob. As Tom followed his orders, Jacob looked at me, shrugged, and said, "What? Because I'm Jewish I can't have an opinion about Christmas lights?"

He leaned over and kissed me on the cheek.

"Hold the ladder still!" Tom yelled down. "And no smooching until Christmas."

"Some holiday spirit," Jacob grumped. Then he added, "Here comes a car!"

Bright headlights flooded the long driveway leading to the house. The passengers didn't seem to notice the three of us, but we all saw this wasn't a car— *it was a red pickup truck.*

"That's Claire! It's Claire!" I yelled. As I ran toward them, I looked back at Jacob and Tom. "It's Claire and Hank and the kids! Hold the ladder tight till Tom gets down. We might need him for the wedding."

I ran as fast as my klutzy Uggs would let me. There they were—Claire and Gus and my precious namesake, Gabrielle, and Toby and . . . Hank was missing.

Then we were huddled together in a noisy group hug—everyone, that is, except Gus, who had that perpetually pissed-off teenage frown on his face.

"Hi, everybody. Claire, what happened to Hank?" I asked as I forced a great big hug on Gus. "Glad to see you, bub," I whispered against his ear.

"Hank couldn't make it. He's so disappointed," Claire said.

I knew that there must be a story attached, but it wasn't the time to ask about it. If Claire wanted to share, she would. For now I was just happy that my "Southern belle" daughter and my grandchildren were here. And I was, I had to admit, a little happy that Hank wasn't with them.

Chapter 37

The family was starting to come together—the great southern contingent had arrived, anyway. And of course, Jacob, Tom, and Marty were here.

"Oh, no, take it away! Take it away from my face!" Toby screamed. With a great dramatic gesture he pushed his dinner plate away. Then he yelled, "No Crazy Tuna Hash for me!"

"Okay," I said. "I'm not the world's greatest cook, but you don't have to hurt somebody's feelings." Toby gave me a hug.

"If we knew you were cooking up the

Crazy Tuna thing, Gaby, we would have driven a lot slower," said Gus. They were the first words he'd spoken since he arrived. I gave him a playful smack on the back of his head, and he chuckled.

"Bunch of comedians," I said, but I was so happy to have them near me. Then I added, "This gourmet delight you baptized Crazy Tuna Hash happens to be the specialty of the house. And since I was all out of canned tuna, I substituted canned salmon."

"Oh, now, that's a big improvement," said Tom, who was pouring red jug wine.

"Listen. Stacey Lee is busy with the food for the wedding, so you're stuck with my cooking tonight. I thought everybody liked this dish."

A silence filled the room. Then everyone burst out laughing.

"Well, the salad is good. And there's nice French bread from Stacey Lee's store," I said. "Now, can I help anybody with more hash?"

"Gaby-Gaby, what exactly goes into

Crazy Tuna Hash?" asked Toby, perfectly innocently, I thought.

"Well, of course, there's tuna . . . or occasionally salmon, if you're very lucky . . . and there's rice, and it involves some cream of mushroom soup, and some Velveeta, and a quarter cup of sherry, and almonds—which I was out of, so I used peanuts—two packages of frozen corn niblets, a can of water chestnuts . . ."

"We've heard enough. Let's stop for a moment," said Jacob. "I think this meal deserves an extra-special grace. Gentlemen?"

Tom stood and said, "Thank you for this meal we are about to receive. It will bring us joy and love and, clearly, it will bring us laughter."

Marty: "We ask for health, for all of us, but especially for Mike, who couldn't be here tonight, but who's coming tomorrow."

And then Jacob: "Finally, we pray for our mother and grandmother and great friend, Gaby. May she find the love and peace she so richly deserves . . . hopefully with me."

As we all laughed and said "Amen," I watched Claire looking at Tom looking at me. Then Claire smiled at me. I didn't know if she was smiling because she thought the prayer was a good one or because she thought she had identified Tom as the groom.

I did know that the kitchen suddenly filled with a blast of cold air. We all looked over at the door.

And what to my amazed eyes should appear? Emily and Bart, of all people.

I rushed over to them. I couldn't believe they'd gotten here two days early. I'd have been grateful if they'd been on time for "Here Comes the Bride."

Dr. Bart—a foot taller than me—looked over my head toward the kitchen table. "Em, this is going to be the best Christmas ever," he said.

"Why's that? The wedding?" Emily asked as she entered the room to hugs.

"No," said Bart. "Because it looks like they're all out of Crazy Tuna Hash."

Chapter 38

It was almost one in the morning, and we were still going strong. I had lit a big fire in the living room fireplace and we'd covered ourselves with quilts and blankets. Even Toby and Gabrielle were wide awake. And Stacey Lee had come by with a pound of her absolutely perfect maple-walnut fudge.

"This fudge is our reward for getting that Crazy Tuna Hash down our throats," said Claire. Everyone laughed and, probably because of the Grand Marnier I was sipping, I laughed too. Actually, I'd served the hash because it was a family joke.

"By the way, I talked to Lizzie a little while ago. She and Mike send their love," I told everyone. The room turned quiet.

Emily said, "I called Liz on the way up. She said Mike is doing better."

"And he is. He's resting up for the rehearsal dinner tomorrow night. And then the wedding," I said. "Plus, he's working on his jokes."

"Well, before I drink any more, I'm going to see how my decorating staff did with the barn," Stacey Lee said and stood up. "I really am bursting to have a look."

"I'll go with you," Marty said.

"Remain seated. No one sees it till it gets my approval," Stacey Lee said, and she left the room by herself.

"I think I'll go for a little walk too," said Gus, who was becoming, if not downright friendly, at least cordial.

"It's cold and it's snowing. Don't go out, honey," Claire said. I was glad to hear her use the word "honey."

"I could use some fresh air," Gus said, getting to his feet. "Too much food."

"You could use a few puffs of weed is what you mean," I said.

"Gaby!" Gus said, acting all shocked and offended. Sometimes he seemed to forget I taught high school.

"Arms out. Legs apart," Marty said as he stood alongside Gus.

"No way!" Gus yelled. "C'mon, Uncle Marty!"

"Then you don't go out," Claire said. "Your choice, dude."

"Give him a break," Bart said. Talk about your good moods. Bart and Emily were like different people. The intense, Type A, New York duo had been replaced by an easygoing, lovey-dovey twosome.

"Nope. This will be quick," Marty said. He began moving his hands over Gus. "Sorry, buddy."

A few seconds later he announced, "Wallet. Mechanical pencil. Gum. Loose change. Gus is clean."

"You're a pervert, Uncle Marty," Gus said.

"So?" said Marty.

"Just a minute," I said. "Hand over the wallet, please."

"Awww, Gaby."

"Hand it over."

I looked inside the billfold section. Sure enough, tucked among a few one-dollar bills was a wrinkled but very fat joint. I took in the wide-eyed concern on Gus's face.

"Nothing in here," I lied. And I handed the wallet back to Gus.

"Sorry," Marty said. "We're on your side, Gus."

"No problem," said Gus. "Anyways, you're right. It's probably too cold to go out."

We watched Tom add a big log to the fire. Toby and Gabrielle were mesmerized by the initial blaze of sparks that the log made. I passed around more fudge. And Bart filled the brandy snifters with a second helping of Grand Marnier. There was something frankly wonderful about having everyone here. Somehow all troubles and cares seemed to diminish when you were with the people you loved.

Then we all distinctly heard *"Ho, ho, ho!"*

Chapter 39

"Ho, ho, ho!" We heard it again.

The sound of two ridiculously happy voices came booming from the kitchen.

"It's Seth and Andie!" Emily said. "They made it!" We rose as a unit, like a tired but reenergized football team, and hurried into the kitchen.

Seth held his hands up in a "stop" gesture. "I know. *You* weren't expecting us tonight. And *we* weren't expecting to be so late. And yes, we are sorry. And yes, we are very cold. And yes, we are very tired . . ."

"But we are also very happy to be here," Andie said.

Then the hugging and kissing officially began. I immediately started apologizing for the lack of food. Then, of course, the Crazy Tuna Hash jokes began all over again. Same jokes too. And thoughts of togetherness kept running through my head. *There's a star rising in the east, and in two days there'll be Christmas and a wedding. And we're here. Together. What could be better?*

"Mom, you with us? Seth to Mom . . . Seth to Mom . . . Come in, Mom," Seth said loudly as he hugged me and twirled me around as if I weighed nothing.

"I'm afraid I was off on a cloud somewhere," I said.

"You're allowed, Gaby," Andie said.

"So, here's what happened," Seth said. "We had a little spinout just outside of Auburn on the Mass. Pike."

"A *little* spinout?" Andie said. "Listen to the writer *spin* his tale. A truck practically flattened us. There could have been a funeral instead of a wedding. But we ended up on the side of the road.

And we were too scared to move. And . . ."

"Andie's exaggerating. Jeez. Everyone knows what a good driver I am."

A chorus of groans rose from the group.

"Anyway, your Crazy Tuna Hash has nothing on us. We were really hungry. So we got off the Mass. Pike in Worcester and had an elegant meal at Taco Bell. I had the new half-pound Nacho Crunch Burrito. Andie, always watching her waistline, had . . . What did you have, my sweetie pie?"

"The Volcano Double Beef Burrito."

"Right. Man, try sitting in a car with her for an hour after that."

"Enough with the frat-house humor," Andie said. "To continue—when we tried to start the car again, the engine was dead. So this nine-hundred-year-old lady—at least I think it was a lady—gave us a jump-start . . . Anyway, it was an adventure."

"Well, here you are," I said. "Here we all are."

Seth looked around at the faces in front of him. "Yep. Here we all are. And in two days Gaby will be marrying somebody in this room. I *assume* it's somebody in this room?"

Silence. Then my grandson Toby piped up: "Well, I sure know it isn't me."

At that moment the kitchen door flew open, and Stacey Lee shouted above our laughter.

"Get your coats on and come out to the barn. You've just gotta see this."

Chapter 40

It had been a wonderful night with our family. And the transformation Stacey Lee had brought to the barn made it even more wonderful.

The splintery old beams had been wrapped in yards and yards of lacey gold-and-white cloth. Evergreen sprays were dotted with holly and ivy and hung from the doors of every stall. The goats and donkey and pig and my white mare looked like they might really be part of a Nativity tableau.

Round tables, each of them big enough for a dozen diners, encircled a raised white dance floor. Each table held bouquets of evergreens and white roses. Hundreds of sprigs of mistletoe hung from the rafters. It would be impossible to walk three feet without inviting a kiss from somebody.

And finally *the lights*—the thousands of sparkling, twinkling white lights that blanketed the walls and the ceiling truly made the scene look like the most exquisite winter night ever. I hugged Stacey Lee.

"How can I thank you?" I said. "In my wildest dreams I never imagined anything this beautiful."

"Honestly, me neither," she said.

"It's like that old line about Venice," Tom said. "It's what God would have done—if He only had the money."

Then I had an idea. I took the cell phone out of my pocket and speed-dialed Lizzie.

"Did I wake you?" I asked, but I didn't wait for an answer. "I hope not, but even if I did, you'll be glad I called. We're all standing in the barn, the barn that Stacey Lee has turned into a Christmas palace. And we're all oohing and aahing and crying and laughing, and I thought . . . well, I'm going to hold the phone up . . . I just wanted you to be here too. And Mike, if he's up."

My singing voice should be called my croaking voice, but I sang "I'll Be Home for Christmas" as loud as I could.

Everyone joined in, including Lizzie on the other end of the phone. Within seconds we were the most beautiful choir in all of New England. The lights sparkled. The old horse whinnied. And my heart filled with such joy it actually hurt. There was nothing like having your family together, especially if you were all friends.

Chapter 41

Like lots of other people in Stockbridge, we counted on the Red Lion Inn for special-event dinners. Graduation parties and sweet sixteens (Emily didn't seem like a sweet-sixteen type, but she couldn't get the gifts without the party), significant anniversaries, and, best of all, those early-autumn afternoons when the tourists had gone back to New York and Boston, and the locals could get a table without a reservation.

It was at the Red Lion that we celebrated the day thirteen-year-old Seth astonishingly had a hole in one. And, leave it to Stacey Lee, the Red Lion was the place she selected to celebrate making her goal at Weight Watchers. "I had fresh fruit for dessert," she always said defensively about that dinner.

So the Red Lion had to be the place for the rehearsal dinner.

I had another reason for choosing it: The food was good, simple fare. At times it seemed that the wedding was turning into a feast of food rather than a feast of love.

The dinner was held in the Rockwell Suite, a big dining room hung with the art of Stockbridge's celebrity, Norman Rockwell. It was billed as a rehearsal dinner, but, as I told everyone, there was nothing to rehearse. I'd done this show before.

The fact was, though, the rehearsal dinner would have almost as many guests as the wedding itself.

Kurt's daughter and son-in-law were here from Burlington. The twins who did odd jobs around the farm, Jonny and Nick Ramiro, asked if they could come. Then there were a few decades' worth of students whom I adored, and who'd sat through my lectures on Emily Dickinson, Fitzgerald, the Brontës, and Stephen King, and the not-to-be-missed "Proper Use of the Hyphen" talk. And so the invitations went out, until the manager at the inn said we had to cap it at one fifty.

Finally, the night arrived.

"Gaby, I owe you, like, a big thank-you," Gus said when he saw me at the door. I assumed he was referring to my lie about his wallet and the marijuana.

"Sometimes a little fib solves more problems than the truth ever could," I said.

"Oh, yeah, that. But I wasn't talking about the joint. I mean, thanks for covering for me. That was cool, but I really want to thank you for not putting me at the kids' table tonight. Really. Seriously. Thanks so much."

"That's because I don't think you're a kid. Now make sure you don't act like one."

He didn't exactly smile at me, but I was pleased that he didn't sneer either. As he turned and walked away I couldn't resist adding, "You know, Gus, it's amazing how a fake velvet jacket from H and M can really dress up a pair of ripped jeans." This time he smiled.

When I looked up, the room was becoming noisy and crowded, exactly what I wanted. All my rowdy friends and relatives in one place.

I was most delighted to see Mike walking in with only a cane. Lizzie had told me that he'd been using a walker around the house, but he was determined to look like, in his words, "a normal person" at the wedding events. I rushed over to him and my strong, wonderful daughter, and we hugged. Then Mike did a little two-step with the cane.

"No tears!" Mike said in a booming voice. "This isn't about my bad luck. This is about your fabulous luck."

"I couldn't agree more," I said. "Tears are for wusses."

Suddenly Lizzie exclaimed: "Oh, sweet Lord, will you look at that!"

Both Mike and I turned to where Lizzie was staring.

I laughed. "Jacob told me he was bringing a 'friend' with him tonight," I said. "I just didn't expect his friend to be breathtakingly beautiful and about half his age. He's trying to make me jealous. And it's working."

"Not the rabbi and the hottie," Lizzie said. "Look at Seth and Andie!"

Sure enough, when I shifted my gaze a little to the right of Jacob, there was Andie with huge plastic antlers on her head, small furry velvet ears, and a huge red nose that lit up. That wasn't all. She wore a brown-and-white sack that made her look like the front half of a reindeer. It came complete with hooves.

As for Seth, red suspenders held up a costume that replicated the rear end of a reindeer. He too had huge brown hooves.

"So, what do you think?" Andie said as she walked, or rather pranced, toward us.

"Pretty cool, huh?" Seth said. "We're such dears, aren't we?"

"Well, as for Seth as the rear end, I'd say it's typecasting," Mike said. "And that's not the last time you'll hear that tonight. Very creative of our star writer and artist from Beantown."

"Lizzie, help me get under here," Seth

said. Then he began burrowing under Andie's part of the costume.

"This seems sort of pornographic," Lizzie said as she pulled the front part of the costume up and over Seth's head. We were now looking at a very lumpy reindeer.

About a dozen friends had gathered around them, and the three-piece band broke into "Rudolph the Red-Nosed Reindeer."

Andie and Seth began dancing immediately, their hooves tapping in nearly perfect unison.

The onlookers broke into applause. I turned to Lizzie and said, "I am so happy I don't have normal children."

Chapter 42

The plot thickened very nicely as the night before Christmas continued.

"I think that Jacob brought this young chick to throw us off the scent," Claire said. All eyes at our table turned to the quite beautiful Amy Stern, Jacob's surprise companion for the evening.

Tom nodded agreement. "Think about it. The very sly rabbi shows up with a date—a fabulous-looking date. So everyone thinks, aha. Let's eliminate him from the list of marriage partners. He's got a girlfriend."

"You think Gaby's so diabolical that

she'd go to all that trouble to confuse the situation?" Seth asked. "You think my mom would do that?"

"I do," said Andie, who had removed her costume's red nose, thus eliminating the possibility of electrocuting herself during the soup course.

"Unless, of course," Marty said. "Unless Ms. Stern *really is* Jacob's date. Then that would mean that someone else—like Tom or me or even someone we haven't thought of—is actually going to marry our Gaby."

"Uh, excuse me, please," I broke in. "If you don't mind, this woman in the red silk dress and sapphire necklace is the person you're all talking about."

There was laughter at the table, but there was also a sense of *"This case has to be solved, Sherlock, and we must do it soon."*

I caught Gus rolling his eyes. When he noticed me noticing him, he did a startlingly accurate imitation of my voice: "Don't let your first time at the grown-ups' table become your last time." He got the inflection, the tone, the style completely right. He had a future, that boy.

While we were laughing, while the soup bowls were being cleared, while a very nice crisp Sancerre was being poured, two missing diners showed up. Full of apologies, only slightly frantic, Emily and Dr. Perfect made their way through the crowd to our table.

"I am so sorry, Mom," Emily said as she kissed me. "We are such idiots."

"Really, we are. We heard everybody leaving the house," Bart said. "And we were all set to go. I was tying my tie, and then . . . I don't know . . ." His voice trailed off.

"I bet I know what happened," Gus said with a high school boy's knowing smirk.

"You know a lot more than you need to know," Claire said as she thumped Gus on the back.

Yes, this was what I was hoping for. The laughs were coming, the wine was flowing, the music was playing. And, of course, the mystery was going strong, stronger than ever tonight. But I didn't have too much time to savor this feeling of joy.

At the front of the room a ridiculous-looking red-nosed reindeer was tapping a glass with a spoon. From the tail of the reindeer emerged a hand. The hand was holding a microphone.

Uh-oh. The toasts were about to begin.

Chapter 43

"Mr. Conductor, if you please" came a voice from the rear of the reindeer. Then Andie and Seth sang the song they were dressed to sing. The tune sounded somewhat like "Rudolph the Red-Nosed Reindeer"—I thought.

**Gaby is getting married
To Stockbridge the family came.
Gaby will have a partner
But nobody knows the name.**

The two of them began dancing on the little raised platform, and the roomful of people were so amused, I decided Seth should cancel the idea of becoming a writer and become a wildly successful party planner.

**She says stop asking questions
She loves this little game
We say stop acting goofy
Tell us the goddamn name!**

Andie and Seth might have had more verses to their song, but they trotted offstage while the audience was still in the palm of their hands—er, hooves.

As the reindeer departed, Lizzie and Mike replaced them. No one had the same hamminess of Seth and Andie, but none of my children or in-laws was particularly shy.

Lizzie spoke first. "Usually, at rehearsal dinners someone stands up and says 'I've known the bride since she was a little girl.' In this case, though, I've got to say I've known the bride since *I* was a little girl. I've actually known her since *before* I was a little girl, since before I was a baby, since before . . . Well, you get the idea.

"Personally, I think the greatest thing of the many great things about my mom would have to be her honesty. She manages to be honest without ever hurting, and that is a talent.

"When other mothers would tell their kids, 'Oh, that vaccination needle isn't going to hurt,' Gaby would say, 'The needle's going to hurt. But it's only going to last a second.' When other mothers would say, 'You look awful in that orange dress. You're too fat for it,' Gaby would say, 'You look wonderful in that orange dress, but, one woman's opinion, you looked even more wonderful in the blue dress with the black jacket.' So, thank you, Gaby, for always telling the truth . . . and never letting me realize how incredibly sneaky and manipulative you were being."

The audience roared.

Then Mike leaned in and said, "Just one more thing. Getting married doesn't mean you stop being the best nurse in town. Keep the lasagna and chicken soup coming. They work a lot better than the radiation."

Tallulah shouted, "Go, Gaby," and I was determined I was not going to cry.

This event was well rehearsed, because as Lizzie and Mike were replaced onstage by Claire, Gabrielle, Toby, and the sourpuss known as Gus, there was "changeover" music—a version of "Away in a Manger" played at breakneck speed.

Claire began, "Most kids present their parents with problems when they're teenagers—drugs, booze, sex, disrespect. I was different. I waited until I was about twenty-three before I did anything like that. I was the perfect teen, but I was a . . . challenged adult. No matter. Gaby was there for me. Always. Every time I needed her, she'd get in the car and make the trip to South Carolina in one day and night. She combined just the right amount of listening with the right amount of persuasive scolding. And if she hadn't, I wouldn't be standing here today with three kids and a job and the ability to run my own life, no matter how rough that turns out sometimes."

Claire raised a glass of water in my direction. "Thank you, Mom. It's your turn now. *Whoever* you're marrying is the luckiest man in the world."

Then Claire looked over at Gus and said, loud enough for all to hear, "If you roll your eyes, it's back to the kids' table for you."

Chapter 44

As Claire and the kids exited left, Emily and Bart entered right.

They looked great together, my lawyer and doctor from the big city. Bart wore a dark black suit, a black shirt, and a dark silver tie. His hair was slicked back in that way that only handsome guys can get away with.

Emily was not to be outdone. She looked like a model. No jewelry (she hated fussy stuff). Her hair was pinned tightly on top of her head—simple and severe, what she called a no-nonsense do. Midlength black skirt. Dark gray cashmere sweater. Black jacket. The only thing about Emily that wasn't high fashion was the big smile on her face.

She picked up the mike and said, "My mom told us not to come dressed as dreary New Yorkers. So!" She signaled the band, put down the mike, and suddenly the music came blaring out at us—"Jingle Bells," played in a bump-and-grind tempo.

Now the show went into another gear.

Emily pulled the pins from her hair, and down it flowed in waves around her shoulders. She removed her jacket, showing bare shoulders and arms. Bart shucked off his jacket. Spun it in the air like a Chippendale dancer and dropped it casually on the floor. Maybe this was how he worked his way through med school?

The catcalls and applause were growing. Emily pulled her sweater up and over her head, exposing a pair of red spaghetti straps attached to a minimal amount of glittery red silk.

When she turned around to show the audience the back, well . . . there was no back. Over to Bart. He unbuttoned his black shirt to reveal a tight, copper-colored T-shirt. He put his black jacket back on, then unbuckled his belt. His black pants fell to the floor, and he was wearing very snug-fitting black-and-white slacks, hemmed so high that the red-and-copper-colored socks momentarily made it look as if he were wearing knickers.

By this time, all eyes were back on Emily. She'd let her skirt drop to the floor. Underneath was the remainder of her dress—a similarly silky, glittery piece of cloth that came to midthigh.

Now Bart picked up the mike. "Like Em said, Gaby warned us not to come dressed as dull working drones from Manhattan," he said.

"I hope we succeeded, Mom," Emily said, giving a little hip bump on "Mom."

The applause was as hot and crazy as the wardrobe. Emily and Bart came to the table for hugs. Within seconds, the whole family was there—grandkids, crazy reindeer, Claire, Liz and Mike (without a cane). Then a chant went up around the room:

"Speech! Speech! Speech! Get up there, Gaby."

"Who, *me?*" said little Gabrielle.

Chapter 45

I took Claire's daughter up front with me, but only for a few seconds and some more laughter as Gabrielle did a little curtsy, then bounded back to her seat.

Then I spoke. "First of all, I've got to thank you all a million times for being here tonight, Christmas Eve—and then coming by tomorrow for the wedding on Christmas Day. If it turns out to be fun, maybe I'll get married every Christmas.

"Now, I know that there's been a lot of speculation as to whom I'm going to marry. The interest has grown so great that I had to turn away reporters from *Entertainment Tonight* and *Us* and *People* magazines. In fact, as late as five o'clock this afternoon, Jay-Z and Beyoncé were on the phone, trying to get an invitation to tonight's dinner. Well, the time has come to tell you who the lucky man is."

Applause and loud cheers from all around the room. "Finally!" somebody yelled. I thought it was Amy Stern, Jacob's "date."

"The time has come," I said, "and that time is tomorrow afternoon." I laughed. A few of the crowd booed, including Tom, Marty, and Jacob.

"Now I have to say a few things from the heart. Violins, please. I've been ending my videos and e-mails and snail mails with the signoff line 'See you at Christmas, and see you in my dreams.' Well, I want you all to know something. The fact is: I always see you in my dreams. I see all my friends over the years. And my favorite students from the high school. I see the folks who help every day with the breakfast and some of those who eat with us every day *at* the breakfast."

I paused. I blinked a few times.

"And I dream about my family. My kids. Their kids. I am forever falling asleep at night and seeing four-year-old Lizzie's fat little legs running away from Pincus the pig. Or watching Seth as a teenager coming home at six in the morning and sneaking through the laundry room window. One day—and this was real life, not a dream—I found myself looking through a cardboard box filled with hockey sticks and baseball gloves made for very little hands. Another time, I was straightening books on the shelf, and I pulled down *Goodnight Moon,* and I recalled how all four of you kids thought this was the finest piece of literature ever written. And then . . . I dreamed that we were all together again for Christmas.

"And here we are. *Just like in my dreams.* And when someone asked me to get married, and then someone else, and so on and so forth, I knew this was a good idea. I knew that the only four people in the world who were nosier than me were my children.

"And it worked! We're all here! The tables are set in the barn. The conductor's ready to strike up the band. Today has been one of the best days of my life, and I know tomorrow will be even better.

"So thank you all for coming this Christmas Eve. Thank you to my wonderful children—Claire and Lizzie and Emily and Seth. Thank you to my incredible grandchildren. And most of all, thank you to—*in no particular order*—Jacob, Tom, Marty, and Stacey Lee. You are the best friends anyone could ever have. I love you, and I know you all love me. Even better, you put up with me. Most of the time.

"Everyone! See you tomorrow. And see you in my dreams!"

Chapter 46

And that was it for Christmas Eve. Well, almost.

The Summerhill family had a drinking-and-driving rule, a rule made many years before. We called it the Double Designated-Driver Rule. All it meant was that there were always *two* people who had to stay sober for driving. So if one of the two drivers decided to refresh himself with an after-dinner cognac, there was always another person ready to take the wheel.

Claire's pickup truck was piloted by Claire herself, who had not had a drink in five years. Seth had offered to drive. He'd stuck to Pellegrino all night, because of our rule, but, as he put it, "If I'm driving and a cop stops us, he's going to think I'm drunk no matter what. C'mon, a car being driven by a guy dressed like a reindeer's ass?"

So Claire did the driving while Seth, Andie, the twins, and I did the gossiping about the evening.

Ten minutes later Claire was pulling into the long driveway at the house. As she shifted into park, I looked out and saw somebody walking toward us. And suddenly I realized that the night wasn't quite over.

"That asshole," Claire said.

It was Hank, of course.

"Am I late for the party?" he said as we got out of the truck. No one answered him.

I had that sense you sometimes get when someone is really good at disguising how drunk he is but you somehow *know* he's drunk anyway. That's how Hank seemed to me.

"Gaby, I understand congrats are in order," he said.

"And I understand there are some rooms at Motel Six in Lenox. I'll get you a reservation and drive you there," I answered.

"Why would I wanna do that when the family is all here?" he laughed.

At that moment Emily and Bart's little BMW came quickly down the driveway. People started climbing out of it as if it were a clown car at the circus—Emily, Bart, Gus, Stacey Lee.

"It's a regular fucking Summerhill family reunion," Hank said. He moved closer to Claire and me. And Seth and Bart moved toward him.

"Ooooh, Dr. Fucking Wonderful and the boy prodigy are here to protect the womenfolk," Hank said. "Think the two of you can handle me? I doubt that very much."

"Take Gaby's advice, Hank," Seth said calmly. "We'll drive you to a motel."

Hank started to shout then, and to wave his arms up and down, and occasionally to leave his feet. "What? And miss the celebration? Miss the miracle that some jack-off is willing to marry this old bag? That somebody, other than you all, is willing to be told what to do and when to do it and how to do it by Gaby? There's . . . there's . . ."

But the words got caught in his mouth, and in a move both sad and infuriating, Hank picked up a rock the size of a child's soccer ball. He threw it with both hands at the pickup's windshield, which shattered and instantaneously looked like a glass spiderweb.

"That's the end of it, Hank," Bart said as he walked quickly toward his brother-in-law. Seth was right next to him. And Gus was next to Seth.

"We're going to get you to the motel," said Bart, who was a big man, after all.

"Don't any of you fucking touch me," Hank said. "I know when I'm not welcome. I get it, I *get* it."

Weeks later when we talked about this evening, everyone said my memory was faulty, but I could have sworn that Hank was crying as he headed toward his little rental car. Before he opened the door, he stopped and shouted.

"Gus!" he said. "Come on and stay with your old man. C'mon, son!"

There was no hesitation on Gus's part.

"Not this time, Dad. Not this time."

Hank fumed, but then he got into the car and began to drive off. He slowed down as he came by us, and the thought crossed my mind that he just might be crazy enough to plow me down. Or that he might have a gun.

But he just stopped next to Claire and me, and he rolled down the window.

"You know, Gaby, let me tell you something," he said. "You're nothing but a phony bitch. Merry Christmas to y'all!"

Then he drove away, and I don't know if we had ever loved him, but we cried for him that night.

Chapter 47

I rarely had trouble falling asleep, but this was no ordinary night. Hank had made it even more, well, dramatic. In six hours we would be serving Christmas-morning breakfast to our homeless friends. And several hours after that I'd be getting married to a very special person. I thought about that person now, why I had chosen him, and how calm and secure I was in my choice. I'd come to believe that if you're going to marry someone, it has to be your best friend, and he was my best friend, somebody I never tired of being around, someone I felt lucky to have love me back. I wished he were here with me right then.

I lay in bed with a nice big snifter of warm brandy next to me. Not surprisingly, Gus knew how to warm Courvoisier to the perfect temperature, and he had done that for me. I shuffled through my big file of wedding notes—menus and bills and checklists for flowers and orchestra and bartenders and, of course, the ever-growing guest list.

Almost everyone in the house stopped by to say good night, and everyone said that tomorrow was going to be a wonderful day. And screw Hank.

I took a sip of the brandy. Mmmmmm. Gus might not have been too good at algebra, but he knew how to fix a glass of Courvoisier.

Then came a barely audible knock at the bedroom door.

"Come on in," I said.

The door opened, and Claire stood there wearing a black silk bathrobe, looking as shy and quiet as she had when she was little.

"Remember this?" she asked.

"I thought I'd given that to Goodwill

the day you moved to Myrtle Beach," I said with a laugh. She turned around, revealing the big silver logo of her favorite rock group when she was in high school—INXS.

"Whatever happened to them?" I asked.

"I think they work in a Walmart in Perth," she said.

I waved for her to come in, and the moment she closed the door it happened—a dam burst. Sobbing. Shaking. Quivering lips. I held out my arms, and Claire rushed to fill them.

"Mom, I've decided something," she said.

"What did you decide?"

"I'm leaving Hank, divorcing him," she said, and then held her head away from me, anxious, I thought, to see my reaction.

After a few seconds she spoke again. "Are you going to say you approve or disapprove?"

"You don't need me to approve or disapprove. A marriage is the most private thing in the world. Only the people in it know if it works for them or doesn't.

All I'm going to say is that I love you like mad."

She sniffled. She smiled. It was a slight, crooked smile, but a smile.

"Thank you. I just didn't want the sad news to spoil your wedding."

"Claire, you're not spoiling anything."

I didn't think it would be appropriate for me to add that she had just given me the best Christmas and wedding gift I could have hoped for.

BOOK THREE

The Christmas Wedding

Chapter 48

Merry Christmas. I just hoped I would live through this day.

A wedding happened to be coming up in several hours, with two hundred or so people attending. I had a farmhouse so full of guests that two of the cousins slept on blow-up mattresses on the kitchen floor.

Well, I must have thought we didn't have enough to do. So, since it was Christmas, it seemed only fair that we have our traditional breakfast for the homeless that morning. I just couldn't say no.

"Mom, a slight planning problem," Seth announced. "The tables in the barn are all set for the wedding dinner. Where will the folks sit? What will they eat with?"

"Seth, a planning solution," I answered. "Let them sit at the beautifully set tables. *It's Christmas.*"

"If Stacey Lee finds out, she'll kill us," he said.

"No, she won't. Because as soon as breakfast is over we're going to wash the china and silver, launder the linen napkins, and get everything back on the tables before the first pig in a blanket is swallowed. Even if I have to do it myself."

Seth nodded as if I had just made perfect sense. He gave me a peck on the cheek and started helping the morning diners find their seats. "As you wish, madame. No one cares for the masses quite like you. Actually, that's true."

Instead of just the regular helpers, my family was pitching in, and certainly not for the first time.

This breakfast was intentionally fancier than most we served. Not the usual oatmeal, fruit, and toast. No, this Christmas morn there were buttermilk pancakes with real maple syrup. Also, scrambled eggs with cheddar cheese and scallions. And every table had a big bowl of sliced strawberries.

I turned and headed toward the big griddle, where Jacob, dapper and handsome, even at this early hour, was flipping pancakes like a short-order cook.

"You're here bright and early," I said. "Slow day at the temple?" He pretended not to realize I was joking. His expression was wide-eyed, and his jaw dropped a bit.

"Gaby, Christmas is not a big day on the Jewish calendar," he said.

As we laughed, Emily walked over, picked up a platter of pancakes, and took off, quick and efficient as ever. "This is crazy, Mom," she mumbled, "but kind of fun." Tom was already at the table with a second platter.

"Thanks for bringing Amy last night," I said to Jacob.

"No problem," he said. "I hope it helped make everyone even more confused. Deepened the mystery. Heated up the plot."

"Oh, I think it did, Jacob. Just the way we planned."

By now, some of the breakfast folks were finishing up. A few regulars stopped by to thank me and wish me a merry Christmas. Almost all of them knew about the wedding that afternoon. In fact, most of Stockbridge knew.

Old Adele Gould came up to me. Miz Gould, as she always demanded to be called, claimed to be eighty, but she was at least ninety. She gave me a feeble hug and said, "God bless you, Gaby. I got married four times, and I loved it."

"You give me great hope and encouragement," I said.

"Miz Gould," I heard a familiar voice say. "I'm in charge of collecting the dirty napkins." It was Marty with a big laundry basket. I hadn't even seen him arrive.

"Fine, go get mine. Right over there." Adele pointed to her near-empty table. She winked at me and departed.

"I guess she knows who the hired

help is," Marty said. We shook our heads and smiled.

"Merry Christmas, Marty," I said.

He bent forward over the laundry basket and kissed me lightly on the lips.

"Merry Christmas, Gaby."

I pulled back a little, surprised. "Marty," I said. "Why do we have tears in our eyes?"

"You're the expert on human nature. I'm just here to wash the napkins. See you later," he said, and walked out the barn door.

Folks were finishing up breakfast. Emily and Bart were washing dishes. Claire was running around with a cloth and a spray dispenser of detergent, rubbing stains out of the tablecloths. Tom had a couple of wastebaskets.

I watched as he gently asked an older lady to please leave the centerpiece on the table. Then he removed a single white rose and handed it to her.

As I walked toward the griddle to clean it, I was cut off by Benny.

I didn't actually recall Benny ever having a last name. He was always "Benny at the gas station," the guy who pumped gas, swept the sidewalk, washed windshields. One thing I did know about Benny was this: He didn't have a single tooth in his head. And he'd happily verify that for you by opening his mouth wide and laughing.

"Gaby," he said. "No one knows who you're marrying, do they?"

"That's not true. I know."

"You're a smart-mouth," he said. Then he looked into my eyes, pretending that he was about to cry.

"Damn it, Gaby. All these years I thought that I was the one you loved."

Chapter 49

After breakfast was out of the way, I retreated to the house. Several hours later, I was desperately trying to make my way through the million and one things I still had to do. A knock came on my bedroom door.

"You want some help getting dressed, Mom?" It was Claire.

"No, thanks. I'm really good at dressing myself. Been doing it for years."

"Okay, wise girl. Yell if you need me. Ninety minutes till takeoff."

Ninety minutes, ninety minutes till the wedding, ninety minutes till the vows, ninety minutes till I did what I had done once upon a time with Peter. Honestly, I couldn't wait, and I had never been more certain that I was absolutely making the right choice for a partner, difficult as that choice had been.

I looked over at the bed, where Stacey Lee had laid out my wedding dress for me. It was only a month before that she and I had driven into Boston to buy it. We had planned on spending the day there, and possibly spending the night with Andie and Seth if we needed another day for more dress or accessories shopping.

Our first stop was the designer floor at Saks in the Prudential Center. The saleswoman showed us a dress designed by Carolina Herrera and made of a purple chiffon so pale that you had to study the cloth to see the purple tint. I remembered hearing a British actress playing a royal role say that when she put on the crown and the robe, she felt she *was* the queen. That morning at Saks I slipped into the chiffon dress and . . . well, I felt exactly like a bride. I clearly saw the wedding reception, the children, the decorated tables, and the man I was going to marry. I was a bride.

When I walked out of the dressing room, Stacey Lee looked as amazed, and delighted, as I felt.

"You look incredible," she said. "Who would have thought that the first dress you tried on would be the perfect one?"

Now that perfect dress lay on my bed, waiting for me to put it on and become a bride.

I slipped it over my head, very, very carefully. It slid down and around my shoulders as if it were made of air. The fashion magic worked. There I was. The bride on her wedding day. I loved the feeling, everything about it.

Oh, yeah. I needed some makeup, especially around my eyes. And I needed some styling gel in my hair, especially on the cowlick that had dogged me all my life. And I needed to change from my New Balance sneaks into something a touch more formal.

I kicked off the sneakers.

I looked in the mirror, and then I turned around. *Yes, ma'am. This dress is perfect. You just might pull this wedding off.*

I practiced taking small steps—not too fast, but not ridiculously slow either. God, I was excited.

I walked barefoot from my reading chair, past the StairMaster, and ended up at the far bedroom window, which overlooked the little stone footbridge that led into the woods, a bridge Peter and I had built years before. Probably on account of my nervousness and happiness, the winter light seemed springtime bright. I wished I could decorate the bare branches of all the trees.

Then I glanced farther down, below the branches. Oh, dear.

There were Tallulah and Gus, crossing the bridge.

An eight-year-old and a fourteen-year-old sneaking into the woods. This was not good. Tallulah looked around nervously behind her. Gus motioned her forward. Then they disappeared.

I took a deep breath. Then I ran down the back stairs and out the side door. This could ruin everything.

Chapter 50

This will sound stupid because it was stupid: I was in such a hurry to follow Gus and Tallulah that I didn't think about being shoeless until I crossed the stone footbridge. Once I was on the other side I stepped into a pile of icy twigs. I let go with the traditional woodland cheer of "Oh, shit," but I wasn't about to turn back. I was sure, however, that in my chiffon wedding dress, a bedroom quilt wrapped around me, and barefoot, I looked like something out of *The Blair Witch Project.*

I had been in these woods a thousand

times. So I knew the layout like a local mapmaker. But it was anyone's guess where those two kids had gone.

I jogged through the orchard of crab apple trees and across the brook over-flow. That area was a mess of mud and wet sand in summer. Today it could have been an ice-skating rink.

I turned onto a dirt path where we often took the dogs for a run, and then . . . *something in the air.* The unmistakable, never-forgotten scent of marijuana.

Following my nose, hobbling on half-frozen feet, I soon saw Tallulah and Gus sitting on a log.

I watched Tallulah take a hit and then cough like crazy. Her mentor, master-class professor Gus, seemed to be giving her directions on how long to hold the smoke in her mouth, how to properly inhale it, and, finally, how to exhale.

"What in hell are you two doing?" I said. "Are you both nuts?"

I was willing to bet that the last time anyone had looked this frightened on Christmas was when Ebenezer Scrooge saw Marley's ghost.

"Gaby!" Tallulah shouted. "What are you doing here?"

"I always like to walk through the frozen woods just before I get married."

"Oh, man," Gus said. "We're fucked."

I walked over to him and pushed him so hard that he fell backward off the log.

"Do you mind? Your cousin is eight years old. Do you mind not using lousy language on Christmas? Do you mind not teaching her how to get stoned? Do you mind not acting like a little punk for once in your life?"

Their joint had fallen to the ground. I saw Gus glance at it.

"Don't you dare touch that thing," I said. "You know, Gus, I covered for you once. I thought you owed me for that. But I guess not. I guess you want to show up at my wedding stoned out of your mind. You don't care if you spoil everything. All you think about is yourself."

"Gaby, that's not it. I just wanted to be mellow for the service."

"And you wanted your eight-year-old cousin to be mellow also?"

He didn't reply. He looked away, and

Tallulah looked down at the ground. After a few seconds Gus spoke again.

"Can I tell you something without you getting angry?"

"Of course you can," I said.

"I just . . . well, let me put it simply: I just love weed."

"You 'love' it?" I asked. There was no anger in me. Probably because Gus was trying to be honest.

"Yeah, when I'm not stoned I think about being stoned. When I'm straight, like in class, I think about when I'm going to be out of class, and then . . ." His voice trailed off.

I waited about half a minute before saying anything. Then I told him, "You know the thing about a love affair? *You can end it.* It's not always easy. And you don't always want to do it. But you *can* do it. And that's what you have to do."

He nodded. He knew me well enough to know that I was a talker, but I wasn't a lecture giver. There was really nothing left for me to say, except "Gus, you're strong. I know you are. You're strong. Stay strong."

Tallulah was still looking at the ground.

She seemed like she might burst into tears, which was okay with me. Her cheeks were already wet.

"And you, young lady. Stick to Skittles and the Jonas Brothers or whoever. And don't hang out with bums like your cousin here." I reached over and hugged her.

"Gaby, watch your dress. It's so beautiful. Don't get it dirty," Tallulah said.

"Come on, you two little criminals. Let's get back to the house. Before long it'll be turning dark. That's all we need to do, get lost in the woods."

Tallulah and Gus stood up, and Gus glanced down at the lonely dead joint.

"Don't you even think about it," I said.

We walked back in complete silence. Tallulah and Gus kept their heads tilted downward. My feet were burning from the cold. The soles were scratched. The toes were numb.

As we got closer to the footbridge, Gus looked down at my feet and almost shouted: "Gaby, how come you're not wearing any shoes?"

"I'm not?" I said. "I hadn't even noticed."

Chapter 51

My poor feet were frozen *and* on fire. If I needed any reminder, there were blotches of blood on the carpet.

I took off my gorgeous dress and examined it for damage and dirt. God was looking down on the bride: The dress was still perfect. But my ripped feet were ready to ruin everything. So I did what I was pretty sure you weren't supposed to do for possible frostbite and bloody cuts—I filled the tub with hot water, sat myself on the edge, closed my eyes, and plopped my feet into the water. It was certainly dramatic.

So dramatic that I let out a yell that brought both Emily and Claire running to the door.

A great deal of banging ensued.

"Mom, are you okay in there?" asked Emily.

"What's wrong? Why did you scream?" asked Claire.

"I'm fine," I said. "Go get dressed."

"What happened? Unlock the door," Claire said.

I noticed little rivulets of blood, a definite pink cast to the bathwater, but I didn't want their help. The fact was, I had one hour until the wedding, and I could barely stand. I should have let those two thoughtless kids get stoned out of their minds. But I couldn't, I just couldn't.

"If you two don't go away immediately," I shouted, "I *will not* let you come to my wedding."

"But are you . . . ?" asked Emily.

"Immediately."

"You're impossible," said Claire.

"Okay, Claire. Now you can't come to the wedding."

"You're impossible," I heard her say

again, but my x-ray vision could see her smile through the door. Emily's too.

I took my feet out of the water and patted them dry with a towel.

Blood was still oozing from the ball of my right foot, and the rest of the skin was significantly scratched. By "significantly" I mean red and raw and bloody and hurting. I covered my feet with medicated powder (I wanted to scream again, but fought the urge). Then I stuck Band-Aids on a few particularly ragged wounds.

Uh-oh. Walking barefoot to my closet was painful.

I took down the box that contained my new Christian Louboutin shoes. I opened the carton, pushed my feet into the shoes, saw stars, and began to cry. If I knew nothing else about what would happen at the wedding, I knew this: I would not be standing in Christian Louboutin heels when I said "I do."

"Mom, are you ready yet?" Seth shouted at the bedroom door.

"Almost," I said. "Leave me alone. I'm collecting my thoughts. Deciding whom to marry." That line almost made me smile.

"Well, come on downstairs as soon as you can. Remember, we're going to have the family toast. Bart's ready to pop the champagne. The kids are in the barn driving Stacey Lee crazy. *Come on down.*"

"Give me two minutes. Make it three."

"Mom, c'mon!"

I grabbed a pair of white ankle socks from a drawer. I was thinking that my ankle-length dress was practically floor-length. If I walked slowly enough, and I hadn't much choice because of the pain, chances were that no one would see my feet.

So I slipped into a pair of white Nikes with purple swooshes on the side.

Purple swooshes. Now, would you look at that? The sneakers actually matched my dress.

Chapter 52

I looked great.

There. I said it. I know it's inappropriate and a little egocentric, but I did have a mirror in my bedroom, and I . . . looked . . . pretty terrific. The dress, of course, was one of a kind, just right, and my butt still appeared to be on vacation. For once my hair and the brush and the blow-dryer formed a nice relationship, so my curls had the right amount of wave and shine to them. The only piece of jewelry I wore was a small diamond solitaire on a gold chain. I'd had it made from the engagement ring Peter had given me many years before.

If the oohs and aahs from my family were any indication, I wasn't completely delusional. I think I'll say it one more time: *I looked great.*

"You look exactly the way they describe brides," Lizzie said. "Radiant and beautiful and . . ."

Emily jumped in. ". . . And young and in love."

Honestly, that was exactly how I felt, and I can't recommend the experience highly enough.

Bart opened the champagne. If ever there was a sound effect for good times, it was the sound of a champagne cork flying off, then bonking against the ceiling.

"Hurry up," said Claire. "Only a half hour to takeoff."

"Why do you keep using that expression, 'takeoff'? It sounds like I'm about to fly to another planet."

"You are," Mike said. "By the way, who's your copilot?"

"Did you really think that trick was going to work?" I asked.

By now all the champagne flutes were filled. Emily lifted hers and looked at me.

"I'm in charge of the family toast," she said. "So, here goes. To Mom. Who spent so much time and effort loving and caring for us. May you now take some of that love and effort and use it for yourself. Good luck. God bless. We love you more than you'll ever know."

A lot of cheering from the home crowd. Smiles all around the room.

"Damn it," I said. "I knew this would happen. I'm going to have to do my mascara all over again."

Then Claire spoke.

"Can I say something?" she asked quietly. Her arm extended into the toasting position, but Claire shook her head as everyone looked her way.

"No, this isn't a toast," she said. "I have an announcement to make. I cleared it with Mom, and she said it was all right to share it with everybody today."

My other children traded confused looks. Claire continued.

"I wanted everyone to know that Hank and I are divorcing," she said.

There were about five seconds of silence. Then an amazing thing happened. Everyone started to cheer and applaud.

"Now, that's wonderful news," said Emily.

"I couldn't stand that surly sonofabitch from the first day he showed up," said Lizzie.

Even Mike had something to say: "You all know me. I like everybody. But I didn't like Hank."

"Enough," I said. "Only good thoughts."

Mike shrugged. "I think dumping Hank was a really good thought."

"You people," I said. "Well, listen. I can't stand around drinking champagne all day. I've got to go fix my eye makeup and then go get married." I paused for just a moment and then spoke directly to Claire. "You made the right decision." My girl smiled at me.

I was walking toward the staircase when I heard Andie's voice. I turned around. She was wearing a gorgeous simple silk dress. A blue hue so pale that you almost had to study it to notice that it even was a color. I could hear my late mother's voice in my head: "There are only three things that you have to be to wear a dress like that—young, beautiful, and a size two."

"Gaby," Andie said. "Seth and I want to talk to you."

"What's wrong?" I asked, feeling a sudden rumble in my stomach that had nothing to do with wedding jitters.

Seth looked at me all too seriously. "Let's go up to your room and talk."

Chapter 53

Andie and Seth were huddled together on the sofa near my makeup table. I sat in my reading chair. This was *their* meeting. But why were we having it now?

"Mom, you know how all my life I've been waiting for something wonderful to happen to me?" Seth said.

"Oh, honey," I said. "If you want to talk about not making the Stockbridge middle-school lacrosse team, let's do it after the wedding."

"Mom. Be serious."

"I'm sorry. I guess I don't want to hear any bad news right now. Go ahead."

"Well, you know how I said we stopped in Worcester on our way up, and how we had dinner—the whole Taco Bell thing? Well, we did stop in Worcester. But we didn't go to Taco Bell."

My matrimonial clock was ticking. "Get to the point, please," I said to Seth.

"Let me tell it," Andie said. "We had made arrangements beforehand to stop at the city clerk's. She promised to wait for us. And she did. We got a Massachusetts marriage license. And, well . . ."

"We were wondering if we could . . ." Seth broke off and started chewing on his lower lip.

Andie jumped in again. "We were wondering if we could get married today too. Reverend Browning knows about it. We told him we had to ask you. Gaby, we don't want to mess things up."

Why was I even trying to wear mascara today? The tears started all over again.

"Oh, you two. Did I hear the phrase 'bad news' come from somebody's mouth during all that explanation? This is the polar opposite of bad news."

We all stood and hugged. And I'll tell you, hugging is a good thing to do on your wedding day. And on Christmas too.

"Who knows about this? Your sisters?" I asked. "Am I the last . . ."

"No. No one. Just you, us, and the minister," Seth said.

"Good. Then let's make it a surprise. Let me do something with my eyes, and then . . . well . . . then we'll all get married."

Chapter 54

Sometimes you talk to a bride a few years or even a few weeks after her wedding, and she says, "I remember nothing. It's all a blur. There was a church, a big reception, and the next thing I knew we were on a beach in Barbados."

Well, it sure wasn't that way for me.

I remember everything, every candle, every flower, every wineglass, every song, every toast, every person who came to the farm. It was as if my brain and my eyes had come together to form the perfect human video camera.

I walked slowly and alone down the aisle. Friends and family waved. Some shouted out. Photographs later revealed that I looked ecstatic, bordering on goofy—a big grin stretched across my face, my eyes as big as apples.

About fifty of my students—past and present—were stationed toward the rear. It was funny what I thought about as I watched them: Janie Creed, whose mother objected so strenuously when I assigned *Portnoy's Complaint* twenty-five years earlier to my senior class. Keshan Saunders, a senior, who never read one of the assignments yet in creative writing submitted an incredibly beautiful sonnet about the death of his grandfather.

Betsey Greenwood, the school principal who'd hired me right out of college, the woman who had said, "You're a fresh one, but you'll calm down. They always do." Now she stood for the second time at one of my weddings, with the aid of a cane.

As I continued my walk I saw folks I'd seen only hours before at the breakfast. Benny blew me a kiss. Adele Gould nodded knowingly. Right next to Adele, the Kuehn twins—Hazel and Suzanne—in their early forties now and still dressing alike. Steve Miller, the pharmacist. Billy, my buddy from the hardware store. And I didn't know who could be waiting tables at the Red Lion Inn—because it looked like every waitress and busboy had taken time off to be here.

Seth was in charge of the music. My only request was that it not be predictable. No Bach cantatas, no "Ave Maria." Then I worried that it might be nothing but Dr. Dre and Eminem. It was neither. Seth had hired a mandolin player and a harpsichordist to play hit songs from the seventies, my high school and college years.

So my slow and easy entrance was accompanied by an exquisitely delicate version of "Seasons in the Sun" and a soft, relaxed rendition of Aretha's "Until You Come Back to Me."

I had almost made it to the makeshift altar. Reverend Browning was standing a few yards ahead, beaming. On one side of him was my family; on the other side were my boys: Tom, Jacob, Marty.

If I was going to cry, it was going to be now. But they all looked so pleased, so calm, that I remained absolutely buoyant.

That is, until I caught sight of Gus. That boy was impeccably groomed, impeccably dressed too. Where had he gotten that beautiful suit?

Then I remembered. The soft gray cashmere suit had belonged to Peter. It was his favorite. Now Gus was wearing it. And I couldn't help it when my eyes filled with tears. Gus looked as handsome as his grandfather, and he was every bit as tall.

By now I was at the front of the assembly of family and friends. I took a deep, quick breath. Then I turned around and spoke.

"Well, so far, so good."

Chapter 55

"I know you all came here for a wedding, but never let it be said the Summerhills don't try to give everybody their money's worth. Rather than just one wedding, we're having *two* weddings this Christmas Day."

A little gasp went up from the crowd.

Seth, wearing a white linen suit and yellow tie, walked from the family group to my side.

Some people looked confused. A few figured it out. Claire whistled, and then Lizzie started everybody clapping.

"Turn and face back toward the house

and you will see the most beautiful bride: my soon-to-be daughter-in-law, Andie."

Andie—her long brown hair flowing over her shoulders—began her own walk down the aisle.

The audience continued to applaud at the surprise.

Andie looked as gorgeous as I had promised. She was wearing what was essentially a sundress—a bright yellow cotton dress with even brighter red poppies, a halter top, tan sandals. She smiled delicately, radiantly.

And in the time it took her to make it to the front of the barn, a cold Christmas Day had turned warm and sweet and full of hope.

When I looked at my daughter-in-law-to-be, I thought: *Andie has a family now, a family who'll love her always. She'll never be alone again.* Andie smiled at me. Maybe she was thinking the same thing.

I took Seth's hands as he passed me on the way to meet Andie. I kissed my son and then I stepped out of the way.

You could barely hear their voices as

they exchanged vows. But they held hands, and nuzzled each other once, and it was just so simple and right. Seth and Andie had known this was the time and the place. When they kissed, everyone started to cheer again. They finally broke apart, and Seth said "We did it" and his voice was cracking, the way it did when he was twelve or thirteen. People say they grow up so fast, in the blink of an eye, and it's so true, isn't it?

The band played a traditional version of "We Wish You a Merry Christmas" as Seth and Andie moved back to join the family group. They were still holding hands.

Now it was my turn, my Christmas wedding—with the perfect man for me.

Chapter 56

How many times had I been inside this old barn? No exaggeration, a few thousand. All those breakfasts with gallons of oatmeal, all those eggs and all that toast and juice. How many times did Peter and I climb the rickety ladders to the lofts to retrieve Christmas gifts hidden from our children? How many times had I gone to one of the lofts and found one of my breakfast friends camping out there?

I was always at peace on this farm, and it made me happy that I was at peace here on this Christmas, my wed-

ding day. A thousand white lights sparkled. Smiles and tears and laughter and
music and flowers were everywhere I
looked.

I didn't want any more drama. Now I
just wanted to get married. So I walked
directly to Stacey Lee and took both her
hands in mine.

I turned and faced the guests. "No,
I'm *not* marrying Stacey Lee. She's just
giving me away!" Laughter followed.
Some wise guy in the band played two
quick beats on the drum.

Stacey Lee and I walked over and
stopped before Jacob, Tom, and Marty.
In those few seconds my mind took a
photograph I knew I would hold on to
forever.

My beloved brother-in-law, Marty,
handsome, sturdy, my friend since before I met his brother. Jacob, with his
carelessly chic stubble and wrinkled
black suit, the gentlest, kindest man I
knew. And Tom, whom I never tired of
talking to, not in all the time we'd known
each other, going back to high school in
Stockbridge and before. Good guys,
every one of them, all good sports.

I gave Tom a kiss on the cheek, whispered "Love you," and then I moved on down the line.

Only Jacob and Marty were left now. At that point, they were both looking a little nervous. Me too, I was quite sure. My hands were quivering, my knees beginning to knock.

I kissed Jacob, whispered "Love you," and then I took Marty's hand in mine. "I love you," I whispered. "I love you so much, Marty. Of course I'll marry you. Who wouldn't?"

A chorus of *awww*s erupted. Then applause. Smiles, laughter, even more applause. Tom and Jacob were clapping too. As I said, great guys, true friends.

But it was Marty I would marry. Who in that barn didn't know and love him? Marty, who plowed snow for everybody who needed his help. Marty, who filled out Medicare forms for widows and widowers. Marty, who didn't know that I knew he was the five-thousand-dollar anonymous donor to the Friends Breakfast fund-raiser every year. Birdwatcher, whale watcher, people watcher—even pretty-girl watcher. The same guy who once punched a drug dealer in Housatonic so hard the thug had to have his jaw wired.

"Take good care of our girl," Stacey Lee said. Then she stepped forward and became my matron of honor.

And Reverend Browning grinned and said, "Well, how about we get these two kids married?"

Chapter 57

This was my vow to Marty that Christmas afternoon:

"Marty, my mother used to say, 'Never get greedy with God.' I think what she meant was 'Don't dare ask for more if you already have what you need.'

"I've thought about this a lot. Life has been generous to me. I've been given a wonderful family, as you can see here today. I had Peter for many wonderful years. I have my health. And this farm. And now I have you. Yay.

"Marty, when you and I talked about

getting married, I wondered, 'Am I getting greedy with God?' And I thought
about it, and then I decided, if you're
given a blessing and you refuse it, that's
just as wrong as asking for something
you don't deserve. It's also a little dumb,
in my humble opinion.

"I love you so much, Marty. I'm so incredibly happy today."

And then Marty said:

"Gaby, I have lived more than half my
life. I don't want to waste another
minute. I want to be with you. Let's get
married."

"Let's get married, Marty."

Chapter 58

Then suddenly, it seemed, we heard the bandleader's voice over a microphone: "Ladies and gentlemen, for the first time as man and wife, here are Gaby and Martin Summerhill." A one-two-three beat exploded, and a song we both loved, "The Way You Look Tonight," filled the room. And we danced.

I loved hearing the applause, and the laughter too. When Marty twirled me, there was an eruption of *ohhh*s. When he dipped me back, there was another exclamation of wonder. People pointed at my sneakers, always good for a laugh. A little more than halfway through our song, Marty leaned in close. "Seth and Andie," he said.

What a sweet, thoughtful man I had married. We slowed down our dancing, like a couple on top of an unwinding music box. Marty held up his hands to stop the applause.

"Ladies and gentlemen, for the first time as man and wife, Andie and Seth Summerhill."

Then the most beautiful newlyweds in the room walked onto the dance floor. They bumped each other like athletes after a victory. Then they stood next to each other and moved their hips and legs and butts in perfect unison as fast electronic music and wacko sound effects filled the barn.

"What song are they dancing to?" Marty asked with a huge grin.

"'Beeper,'" I said. "By the Count and Sinden."

"You know this song?" Marty was completely amazed.

As I nodded, I failed to add that I knew it only because Andie and Seth had told me about it earlier when we kind of planned to share the dance floor—even before Marty thought of it. As my mother used to say, "Don't tell your husband everything, only the important things."

Chapter 59

The most familiar wedding rituals can transform themselves into meaningful traditions when it's your wedding. The tossing of the bouquet, dancing with relatives you haven't seen in years, the achingly embarrassing toasts . . . I wanted it all, and I loved every minute of this Christmas wedding.

It was time for the bride and groom to dance with everyone else—in a sort of descending royal order.

So, after Andie and Seth finished amazing the crowd, after the band-leader announced that they could next be seen on *Dancing with the Stars,* after the music changed into a Cole Porter–Billy Joel recital, the dancing continued. I danced with Seth. Marty fox-trotted Andie around the floor.

Then Marty and Claire danced. Then Marty and Lizzie.

By the time I was swaying to "Time After Time" in the arms of Jacob, Marty was holding little Gabrielle on one strong arm and Tallulah on the other. Quite the memorable image.

I danced with Toby, who hugged my legs. I danced with Tom, then with Jacob, and they both told me I was forgiven, and even that I'd made the best choice.

A few minutes later, when Marty and I were walking back to our table, someone tapped him on the shoulder and said, "May I have this dance with your wife?"

We turned around. It was Gus.

"Okay, but I'll be watching you, mister," Marty said. "Don't think you're going to try any smooth country-boy moves on my girl."

Gus and I found a place on the floor

up near the band. I was astonished: The boy really knew how to dance—right hand on my back, left hand slightly extended and holding mine. My left hand rested on Gus's shoulder, on the plush cashmere of Peter's old suit. I brushed it gently. I moved my face an inch or so closer to the material. Then I whispered, "Thank you."

Gus looked confused. "Do you want to stop dancing?" he asked.

"Stop?" I said. "Gus, I've just begun."

Chapter 60

I was so distracted and happy that I didn't even notice the stabbing pains in my feet. But I did feel relieved when Marty and I sat down. Most of us at our table—Marty, myself, Andie, Seth, Jacob, Tom, Stacey Lee—hadn't eaten since breakfast. I practically vacuumed down the salmon and caviar appetizer. Totally delicious.

"Have you seen the final menu?" Stacey Lee asked, leaning over my shoulder.

After our food-testing session, where our crack team of gourmets hadn't been able to eliminate a single one of the choices, I had given Stacey Lee total freedom in planning the wedding dinner. Why not? She knew a lot more about party planning than I did, and I had enough other things to worry about. I guessed that with the first course through, I might as well look at the menu.

I picked up the heavy vellum card next to my water glass and read:

Hors d'Oeuvres Variés
Smoked Scottish Salmon with
Beluga Flan
Wild Mushroom Bisque
Salad of Lamb's Lettuce and
Heirloom Tomatoes
Choice of
Crazy Tuna Hash
or
Crazy Chicken Hash
Assorted Petits Fours
Wedding Cake

As you might imagine, the main-course choices came leaping out at me. "Are you crazy?" I said to Stacey Lee. I showed the menu to Marty, who started laughing.

As if on cue, a waiter placed in front of us the most beautifully composed plates I'd ever seen—an elegant pyramid of pieces of fresh tuna resting on a bed of fingerling potatoes, all of it topped by a cream sauce with shallots and toasted almonds.

"Enjoy," Stacey Lee said as she returned to her seat.

Chapter 61

"I don't want one of those cliché wedding photos where the bride puts way too much cake in the groom's mouth," Marty said. It was time to cut the wedding cake, a huge chocolate creation shaped like a barn.

"Maybe a slice that's just a *bit* too large," I said. "That'd be okay, right?"

"Gaby," he said, a note of warning in his voice.

We were leaving the family table when Claire shouted out, "Not too big a piece, Mom. You don't want him to choke."

"Just what I said," Marty called back.

Then my eyes went to Lizzie and Mike. Mike's head was bowed, and Lizzie was massaging the back of his neck. Something wasn't quite right.

By the time I walked the few feet over to them, Bart was standing next to Mike. He was taking his pulse. Suddenly I saw that Mike was beginning to shake.

Marty, Lizzie, Bart, and I gathered around Mike. The people in the barn quieted. Whispers. Questions. The music stopped.

Mike's right arm shot up and out of Bart's grip. Then his legs went stiff.

"Help me lay him down on the floor," Bart said to Marty.

They did that, and I shoved a bunch of crumpled napkins under his head. Now both Mike's legs were lifted a few inches above the floor. The big barn was almost completely silent now.

"Okay, buddy. It's going to be okay," Bart said. It was the first time I'd ever seen his bedside manner, and it was pretty impressive. "Just stay alert. Stay with me here. That's great, Mike. You're fine. Hold on to me."

Mike's eyes rolled up and back. His

eyelids closed. His right leg shot up and down like an automated lever that had been broken.

Then calm came over Mike, and that was even scarier.

"Let him just stay here for a few minutes," Bart said. "He's doing fine. The storm's passed."

Lizzie rubbed Mike's shoulder gently. Tallulah knelt at her father's head. Then Mike finally opened his eyes, as if he'd just been sleeping there in the middle of the wedding reception.

"What the hell did you put in that champagne, Gaby?" he said, and he tried hard to laugh.

After another five minutes or so, Marty and Bart got Mike up and into a chair.

"How you feeling, Big Mike?" Marty asked.

"I'll make it through the dessert course," he said.

"I think we should get you to the hospital. Are you strong enough to walk?" Bart asked.

"I can walk. But no fast dancing. A waltz would probably be okay."

Marty and Bart hoisted Mike to his feet. Then they walked him slowly toward the barn doors.

"I'll go with you," Lizzie said.

"No need to," said Marty.

"Yeah, no need to, sweetie," said Mike. "I know how much you love wedding cake. Have a piece for me."

They continued to walk to the door. When they got there, Bart turned to the crowd and called out, "Enjoy the party. Mike's going to be fine."

Chapter 62

Suddenly I felt uncomfortable in my wedding dress. The thousands of white lights looked overdone. The band played, but no one was dancing. I was sitting at the family table, holding Lizzie's hand. So was Tallulah.

"What are you thinking?" I asked her. "Talk to me, Lizzie."

"I'm thinking that Mike's going to be so embarrassed that he caused this big commotion," she said.

"If I hear an apology, from you or Mike, I'm going to do something I never did when you were a child."

"Hit me?" she asked.

"Very hard," I added. Lizzie smiled and said, "I'll be right back. Stay with Tallulah."

As Lizzie walked toward the barn door, a waiter asked me if I wanted more coffee. "Only if you put a stiff shot in it," I replied.

"Whatever you say. You're the bride."

In a moment, Lizzie returned.

"Uncle Marty's car is still there," she said. "I can't find anybody."

"Maybe they went to the hospital in Bart's car. I'm sure that's it."

I drank my brandy-spiked coffee. It warmed me. I thought how glad I was that Marty was with Mike and Bart. And then—

A crash of cymbals. A loud staccato beat of drums. A trumpet blare. Then suddenly the band was playing "For He's a Jolly Good Fellow."

I spun around, and to my amazement I was looking at Marty, Bart, and Mike walking back into the barn. All three of them were smiling.

Mike gave a small wave to the crowd.

Lizzie and I practically ran a race to his side.

"Didn't you go to the hospital?" Lizzie asked.

"Apparently not," Mike said as he kissed his wife and then leaned in to receive a hug from Tallulah, who had joined us.

"There's nothing they could do for him at the hospital that we couldn't do here," Bart said.

"Like what?" I asked.

"Like have him relax a little, rest a little, and have a nice big glass of Coke."

By this time several more members of the family had gathered around Mike. He was clearly touched by everyone's concern. How did I know that? The tears in Mike's eyes were a dead giveaway. Also—no jokes for the moment.

"I knew you couldn't stay away from our weddings," Seth said as he gave Mike a hug. Then Andie put her arms around her new brother-in-law, and as I watched the warmth in her eyes and the tenderness in her touch, I knew she was now officially a part of the family.

"I'm sorry for stealing the limelight,

Gaby," Mike said. "But—that's what I do."

The band was striking up "The Bride Cuts the Cake." I had forgotten all about the crazy ritual.

"I think we're wanted back at the cake stand," Marty said to me, "unfortunately. Nice try, Mike."

Mike put his hand on Marty's shoulder. "Thank you for everything. I don't know what I would have done without you and Bart."

Marty and I took each other's hands and walked to the center of the barn. I purposely cut a huge hunk of cake and slid the silver cake server under it.

"Don't you dare do that, Gaby."

So I cut a much smaller piece. I held his chin with one hand and put a perfectly sized portion of cake in his mouth. Marty returned the favor, and as I was savoring Stacey Lee's magnificent concoction of chocolate cake, mousse, and chocolate ganache, the crowd applauded. The band played on.

And I watched Gus and Tallulah slip out the side door of the barn. Oh, I just couldn't believe it.

Chapter 63

I moved very quickly toward the side door. This time I was lucky enough to be wearing sneakers. I made it to the foot-bridge in really good time. Plenty of moonlight. But there was no sign of Tal-lulah and Gus.

I finally turned back toward the house, and I heard voices. But the voices weren't coming from outside, and they weren't coming from the woods. In fact, they seemed to be com-ing from inside the main house. Maybe somebody had wanted to get away from the noise of the party. Maybe somebody wanted to rest on a sofa. But maybe it was Gus and Tallulah.

I stepped onto the back porch. No voices now. I ventured into the empty kitchen. Still no voices. The mystery deepened. In the hallway I could hear stage whispers from upstairs. Gus and Tallulah. Damn them.

The stairs creaked with age. My brilliant solution? I took them two at a time.

When I got to the landing I heard the voices clearly: They were coming from the little room next to the master bedroom, the room I used as an office.

Instead of rushing in like a crazy person, yelling "Aha!," I slowly, softly, and carefully opened the door. Tallulah and Gus were at my desk. The printer on the nearby table was churning out pages. To my surprise, there was no smoke in the air, no sweet smell of pot.

Tallulah saw me first. "Oh, my God!" she shouted. "It's Gaby!"

Gus spun around and positioned himself in front of the printer, the printer that was turning out a small mountain of papers.

"Hey, shouldn't you be with your guests?" he asked. "With Marty?"

I threw him a suspicious glance, ignored the questions, and said, "What exactly are you two doing?"

"Bet you thought we were in here smoking dope," Gus said. "Am I right?"

"Don't you want to be surprised?" Tallulah asked.

"I'm sure that, whatever it is, I'll be surprised," I said, and Gus finally handed me a sheet of paper.

"It's something we're giving to every guest when they leave," Tallulah said.

What they'd handed me was testimony to computer creativity and Photoshop. There I was with my arms extended. Holding on to one arm were Lizzie, Claire, Seth, Emily, Bart, Mike, and Andie. On the other arm was Marty. At the top of the page was the headline "JUST ONE MORE TO LOVE!"

It was incredible—touching and real (although why they used a photo of me in a turquoise T-shirt I'd never understand).

"This is sweet," I said. "But why'd you wait until the last minute?"

"Duh, maybe because we didn't know *who* to put on your left arm," Tallulah said.

"Yeah," said Gus, as he handed me two other sheets of paper. "We had to be prepared for anything. Maybe even Benny at the gas station. Ha ha."

On these two sheets the picture of me and the children remained the same, but one had Tom as my marriage partner and the other Jacob.

Marty appeared at the door. "What's going on?" he asked.

"Look at this wonderful photograph," I said, making sure to hand him the sheet that featured him.

"Incredible," he said. Then he grabbed my hand and said, "We should get back to our wedding."

"Thank you both," I said, hugging Tallulah and Gus.

At the door, Marty turned and asked, "How'd you know I was going to be the groom?"

Tallulah shrugged, but with Gus there was always a comeback.

"Lucky guess."

Chapter 64

For Marty and me, and Andie and Seth, it was like no other wedding ever. Still, the celebration ended just like any other. The musicians slipped their instruments into their cases. The caterers collected stray glasses and napkins. Guys in jumpsuits folded up the wooden tables. The old barn was becoming the old barn again. Except for all those twinkling white lights.

Tom left early but not before he came and gave both Marty and me high-fives and congratulations. "I was second, right?" he said.

"Tied for second."

Lizzie and Mike waited for the crowd to disperse before they walked over to Marty and me. I was pleased to see color in Mike's face, and while I couldn't say that there was a spring in his step, he seemed to be walking okay and definitely to be feeling better. Leave it to Emily to know we needed a doctor in the family, her Bart.

"Thank you both for everything," Marty said.

"I didn't do much," said Mike with a shrug. "All I really did was stay alive."

Lizzie gave him a slap and said, "How long can I stand this gallows humor?"

"A long time, I hope," said Mike.

"We'll come by tomorrow to pick up Tallulah—late morning," Mike said.

"Make that early afternoon," said Marty.

"Oh, you crazy newlyweds!"

Seth and Andie stood talking to Claire and Jacob. Then they all walked over to say their good-nights.

"It was a *nearly* perfect wedding," Jacob said with a grin. "You missed by some whiskers." Damn, he was funny. I hoped this wouldn't change anything between us. I didn't think it would. Jacob was a big-picture guy, after all.

Finally Andie and Seth were the only ones left besides Marty and me—the four newlyweds.

Andie took my hands in hers. "Thank you so, so, so, so much, Gaby. You're always so generous."

I laughed. "What's an extra wedding or two?"

"I'm going to grab our knapsacks, and then we're heading back to Boston," Seth said.

"Don't drive all that way now," Marty said. "Stay the night."

"No," said Andie. "We're so hyper we couldn't possibly go to sleep."

Then Seth said in a loud whisper, "Plus, I reserved a suite at the Copley Plaza."

"You didn't," shouted Andie.

"I did." A pause. Then Seth said, "I love you, Mom."

I nodded. "I love you too. My favorite son."

Moments later Marty and I turned and surveyed the empty barn. A chicken squawked. An owl landed on a rafter. Everything was as it had been—except it was still Christmas, and Marty and I were married.

He took my hand. Then he kissed me softly on the lips, and he was a really terrific kisser. Gentle and firm and just right. Part of his charm, part of the attraction.

"You know, it's late," he said.

"I know." But we didn't head for the house right away. Instead, I rested my head on his chest and Marty started to hum our song, "The Way You Look Tonight."

And we danced in the magical glow of the twinkling lights, and I couldn't have been happier. Believe it or not, that happens sometimes.

GABY'S LAST VIDEO

Obviously we're home from our whirlwind honeymoon. I'm happy to report that it was perfect, just perfect. I assume you all remember this handsome man seated to my left.

And yes, Paris, Rome, Florence, and Venice are as beautiful as they were when I visited them the year I got out of college.

Anyway, it's good to be home. Marty agrees. I'm back to school tomorrow, and I hope that substitute teacher taught *Moby-Dick* these past couple of weeks. I never could stand that long-winded tome, though I admire it.

Well, it looks like a few important things happened while Marty and I ran around Europe. It all sounds good or almost good.

First, and most important, there's Mike. He's working at the hardware store four days a week. He told me that he takes weekends off because he's still not strong enough to face all the do-it-yourself people who show up on Saturday to ask a million questions. Beyond that, he had two MRIs last week, and things look promising. The doctors won't use the word "remission" yet, but they said they might use it if the next MRI looks the same. I'll assume that those candles I lit in Notre Dame Cathedral helped at least a little.

Down in New York, Emily took about an hour off for vacation, then immediately got a job working for the state attorney general, investigating Medicaid fraud. All I can say is that I hope her husband, the eminent neurologist, watches his step when he sets up practice. Emily does not play favorites.

There is also some news out of Boston, where the other newlyweds are frolicking. Now they have another reason to rejoice. I'll get right to it: Farrar, Straus and Giroux bought Seth's novel. Of course, they want a million changes, and, of course, they don't have a release date, and, of course . . . well, who cares? They bought it! So now he and Andie are going to get to work on their children's book . . . and . . . all's well that ends well.

Last, and certainly not least, Claire, Gus, Gabrielle, and Toby have moved to Stockbridge. This is indeed good news. Next year, Gus will be attending Stockbridge High, where I will be watching over him myself.

I guess that's it for now.

Oh, yes. One other thing.

Marty and I couldn't be happier.

Thank you all for being a part of this adventure—like no other, I suspect. I don't know what we would have done without you. Seriously, that's it for now. I've got to go sort through the mail, then we'll have a little bit of wine, then I'll see what lesson I have to teach tomorrow, then I'll make sure we have enough food for the breakfast tomorrow, then . . .

Hold my hand, Marty. Hold it tight. You're such a doll.

[Camera moves to Marty:] I am a doll, aren't I. You're a lucky girl.

I don't have the slightest idea why I'm starting to cry. Maybe because I *am* the luckiest girl in the world. Our family has had its share of heartbreak and failure, of sickness and death, but we always have each other.

So I'd better stop talking.

Oh, wait. There is one last thing I wanted to say . . .

See you next Christmas, and see you in my dreams.

Yay.

About the Authors

James Patterson has had more *New York Times* bestsellers than any other writer, ever, according to *Guinness World Records.* Since his first novel won the Edgar Award in 1977, James Patterson's books have sold more than 240 million copies. He is the author of the Alex Cross novels, the most popular detective series of the past twenty-five years, including *Kiss the Girls* and *Along Came a Spider.* Mr. Patterson also writes the bestselling Women's Murder Club novels, set in San Francisco, and the top-selling New York detective series of all time, featuring Detective Michael Bennett.

James Patterson also writes books for young readers, including the award-winning Maximum Ride, Daniel X, and Witch & Wizard series. In total, these books have spent more than 200 weeks on national bestseller lists, and all three series are in Hollywood development.

His lifelong passion for books and reading led James Patterson to launch the website ReadKiddoRead.com to give adults an easy way to locate the very best books for kids. He writes full-time and lives in Florida with his family.

Richard DiLallo is a former advertising creative director. He has had numerous articles published in major magazines. He lives in Manhattan with his wife.

Books by James Patterson

FEATURING ALEX CROSS

Cross Fire • *I, Alex Cross* • *Alex Cross's Trial* (with Richard DiLallo) • *Cross Country* • *Double Cross* • *Cross* • *Mary, Mary* • *London Bridges* • *The Big Bad Wolf* • *Four Blind Mice* • *Violets Are Blue* • *Roses Are Red* • *Pop Goes the Weasel* • *Cat & Mouse* • *Jack & Jill* • *Kiss the Girls* • *Along Came a Spider*

THE WOMEN'S MURDER CLUB

10th Anniversary (with Maxine Paetro) • *The 9th Judgment* (with Maxine Paetro) • *The 8th Confession* (with Maxine Paetro) • *7th Heaven* (with Maxine Paetro) • *The 6th Target* (with Maxine Paetro) • *The 5th Horseman* (with Maxine Paetro) • *4th of July* (with Maxine Paetro) • *3rd Degree* (with Andrew Gross) • *2nd Chance* (with Andrew Gross) • *1st to Die*

FEATURING MICHAEL BENNETT

Tick Tock (with Michael Ledwidge) • *Worst Case* (with Michael Ledwidge) • *Run for Your Life* (with Michael Ledwidge) • *Step on a Crack* (with Michael Ledwidge)

OTHER BOOKS

The Christmas Wedding (with Richard DiLallo) • *Kill Me If You Can* (with Marshall Karp) • *Now You See Her* (with Michael Ledwidge) • *Toys* (with Neil McMahon) • *Don't Blink* (with Howard Roughan) • *The Postcard Killers* (with Liza Marklund) • *Private* (with Maxine Paetro) • *The Murder of King Tut* (with Martin Dugard) • *Swimsuit* (with Maxine Paetro) • *Against Medical Advice* (with Hal Friedman) • *Sail* (with Howard Roughan) • *Sundays at Tiffany's* (with Gabrielle Charbonnet) • *You've Been Warned* (with Howard Roughan) • *The Quickie* (with Michael Ledwidge) • *Judge & Jury* (with Andrew Gross) • *Beach Road* (with Peter de Jonge) • *Lifeguard* (with Andrew Gross) • *Honeymoon* (with Howard Roughan) • *Sam's Letters to Jennifer* • *The Lake House* • *The Jester* (with Andrew Gross) • *The Beach House* (with Peter de Jonge) • *Suzanne's Diary for Nicholas* • *Cradle and All* • *When the Wind Blows* • *Miracle on the 17th Green* (with Peter de Jonge) • *Hide & Seek* • *The Midnight Club* • *Black Friday* (originally published as *Black Market*) • *See How They Run* (originally published as *The Jericho*

Commandment) • *Season of the Machete* • *The Thomas Berryman Number*

FOR READERS OF ALL AGES

Witch & Wizard: The Manga, Vol. 1 (with Svetlana Chmakova) • *Daniel X: Game Over* (with Ned Rust) • *Daniel X: The Manga, Vol. 2* (with SeungHui Kye) • *Middle School: The Worst Years of My Life* (with Chris Tebbetts, illustrated by Laura Park) • *Maximum Ride: The Manga, Vol. 4* (with NaRae Lee) • *ANGEL: A Maximum Ride Novel* • *Witch & Wizard: The Gift* (with Ned Rust) • *Daniel X: The Manga, Vol. 1* (with SeungHui Kye) • *Maximum Ride: The Manga, Vol. 3* (with NaRae Lee) • *Daniel X: Demons and Druids* (with Adam Sadler) • *Med Head [Against Medical Advice teen edition]* (with Hal Friedman) • *FANG: A Maximum Ride Novel* • *Witch & Wizard* (with Gabrielle Charbonnet) • *Maximum Ride: The Manga, Vol. 2* (with NaRae Lee) • *Daniel X: Watch the Skies* (with Ned Rust) • *MAX: A Maximum Ride Novel* • *Maximum Ride: The Manga, Vol. 1* (with NaRae Lee) • *Daniel X: Alien Hunter* (graphic novel; with Leopoldo Gout) • *The Dangerous Days of Daniel X* (with Michael Ledwidge) •

Maximum Ride: The Final Warning •
*Maximum Ride: Saving the World and
Other Extreme Sports* • *Maximum Ride:
School's Out—Forever* • *Maximum Ride:
The Angel Experiment* • *santaKid*

For previews of upcoming books and more
information about the author, visit
JamesPatterson.com or find him on
Facebook or at your app store.